Stasis

Edited by Libby Graham

Stasis

AN ANTHOLOGY OF RETROFUTURISMS

EDITED BY
LIBBY GRAHAM

bellpressbooks.com
Twitter: @bellpressbooks
Instagram: @bellpressbooks

ISBN 978-1-7387167-5-3 (print) | ISBN 978-1-7387167-6-0 (ebook)

Edited by Libby Graham
Cover art by Justicia S
Copyediting by Devon Field

LIBRARY AND ARCHIVES CANADA CATALOGUING IN PUBLICATION
Title: Stasis : an anthology of retrofuturisms / edited by Libby Graham.
Other titles: Stasis (Compilation)
Names: Graham, Libby (Editor), editor.
Identifiers: Canadiana (print) 20240516834 | Canadiana (ebook) 20240520513 | ISBN 9781738716753
  (softcover) | ISBN 9781738716760 (EPUB) | ISBN 9781738716777 (Kindle)
Subjects: LCSH: Science fiction. | LCSH: Short stories. | LCGFT: Science fiction. | LCGFT: Short
  stories.
Classification: LCC PR1309.S3 S73 2024 | DDC 823/.0876208092—dc23

Bell Press publishes and operates on the unceded Coast Salish Territories of the Musqueam, Tsleil-Waututh, and Squamish peoples.

Contents

Introduction

It is easy to look around at the world and freeze, even without the help of a cryogenic sleeping pod. I often feel as disoriented as characters in books and films when they wake from stasis—alive in the same body, aware in the same mind, but thrown into an altogether unfamiliar world.

We are constantly told to learn from the past, live in the present, and look to the future. Science fiction is uniquely suited to hold these often-opposing concepts in harmony. This collection explores not only the changes in science fiction as a genre, but also the wider political and societal shifts that have occurred since its inception. It is especially interested in the way the aesthetics of the past influence our current perceptions of the future.

In the mid-20th century, sci-fi was often used as a tool to express anxieties over nuclear war, the space race, and the principal alien "other"—communists. These stories were predominantly written by Western white men, whose identities aligned with dominant norms. Pulp sci-fi featured heroic (white) men saving vulnerable (white) women from the terrifying grasp of (racialized) alien foes. Colonialism, racism, sexism, and a plethora of outdated ideals have been frozen into the popular imagination of science fiction.

Stasis explores our shifting anxieties, the lenses with which we see them, and the tool of science fiction as a means to express them. It also leans into the idea of science fiction as a leading literary frontier for experimentation, as independent science fiction magazines and small presses carve space out for peoples historically—and continually—removed from the conversation.

What might our future look like stripped from patriarchal rule? Who benefits from the art of resistance? How do we engage with community in the face of climate disaster? These are just some of the questions asked in the stories of *Stasis*.

Stasis will transport you to different times and different worlds. As you read these stories, I invite you to reflect on the time in space we occupy, and where in the world we might be going next.

Libby Graham, editor

Space Diner Coconauts

by Roxane Llancue

Cherrie Limón had always loved to collage stars. The moment she received her license, she had taken the winnings from her coconut booth, stolen her brother's car, and driven all around New Mexico in her hunt for photographs, paintings, and any depiction imaginable of the celestial bodies above her. Their bright lights were her reprieve from the grim existence her family carved out in scrap metal. When she and her brother, André, were scavenging junkyards at night, Cherrie would look up to the sprinkled sky above and dream of seeing them up close, of drifting between planets and meeting those aliens said to have crashed in her hometown of Roswell.

Chicanos were alien to most gringos, so wouldn't it stand to reason they might find more kinship with the extraterrestrials?

It was only after the fabled crash incident that her family took interest in her passion and began to build their Space

Diner in Roswell based on her designs. Her parents ransacked her drawings and collages, and with their last penny opened the UFO-shaped diner to astonishing success. They had Cherrie and her friends dress up as aliens and offer their Space Shakes to the endless crowds of young men coming to find out the truth about the crash, Cherrie trying her best to keep the blueberry and coconut water from spilling under the constant onslaught of their grabbing hands.

Now, Cherrie sucked the last sip from the coconut in her hands with a satisfied smile as she sat up from the cockpit seat and looked over the controls to the glowing blue of Earth—they were orbiting at an angle that revealed the shape of North America just so. Pride straightened Cherrie's back as she let her hands glide over the beautiful controls of the crème and cranberry cockpit Gill had built to her wishes. What had once been a flamboyantly designed bar was now the stunning navigation center of a Space Diner flying through space—an allocation of buttons and levers of gold and titanium that had lifted them above everything.

Their baby had come home.

Arrived among the stars, Cherrie found herself collaging images of Earth for the first time: aquarelles of her ramshackle family home, sketches of the junkyards flung with the brutal beauty of asteroid fields from her hands onto paper. Her coal-smudged fingers gently traced the portraits of her family in her scrapbook wedged between the controls, captured next to eerie Mexican landscapes she had never seen with her own eyes.

With a sigh, Cherrie turned to the TV receiver. She fiddled with the buttons until the news report from Earth flickered alive, black and white amidst the vibrant colors of their ship.

"—the military still scrambling to explain the second Roswell Incident that has shaken the nation. The Airforce has confiscated alleged footage of Roswell's Space Diner taking off to the skies and continues to categorically deny its authenticity. But there is no trace

Pictures of the Space Diner when it was anchored to Earth flickered over the screen, followed by footage of the steaming crater left in its place, policemen forcing back the mass of onlookers. Pictures of Cherrie in her alien uniform followed and she wrinkled her nose at the sight: her perfectly styled hair, her forced million-watt smile, and the unhappiness in her dark eyes.

"—nor of the diner's regular Gillian Ross, the disgraced former physics prodigy and one of America's first female space engineers. Ross was ousted from her military-adjacent position under the law of President Eisenhower's Section 8, signed to rid our government of sexual deviants—"

Cherrie's frown softened at the sight of her girlfriend's photograph, one of the many she had defiantly taken in overalls, her strawberry-blond hair flowing untamed over her shoulders, spots of oil on them that matched the sparkle of her intelligent eyes.

"Te extraño." She traced her fingers over the screen with tenderness.

"—and although Limón's family fervently denies it, rumors of indecency between the two missing women persist. Ross, described both as a genius and a madwoman, is charged with the theft of military-owned titanium. Witnesses claim to have observed her drawing 'spaceship blueprints' in the diner, giving ground to a wild theory—"

Cherrie's head snapped up when she caught new movement out the window and broke out into a giant smile when she saw the cloud nearing their ship. She quickly administered the sequences Gill had taught her and ran out of the control room, the news report following her weakly.

"—some going as far as to question whether these ladies are even members of our human race, for how could two young women have accomplished such a feat as space travel—"

Cherrie practically skipped to the docking chamber, pulling her turquoise suit and helmet on and pressing her hands against the small window in the hatch where she watched the cloud getting closer and closer.

"—reporters have begun referring to the women as 'Space Coconauts,' a name taken from—"

Cherrie almost tumbled with the tremor of the life shuttle docking onto the ship but pulled herself upright with a laugh, the swirling cloud camouflage of the craft and her anticipation making her dizzy with joy. When Gill had told her she wanted to implement her crazy drawing into reality, she had thought her brilliant partner was joking. But she made it a glorious reality, and it seemed Gillian Ross had evaded the eye of the American war machine once again.

The cloud illusion evaporated, and the shuttle's door opened, revealing the lanky figure of her suited girlfriend. Cherrie held her breath as she watched her reach the compression chamber. Two heartbeats, one, and they fell into each other's arms.

After squeezing her as close as humanly possible, Cherrie ripped the offending helmet off, palmed the freckled, smiling cheeks, and pulled her lover into a searing kiss.

Her Gillian was home.

After she had cuddled and caressed her not nearly to her heart's satisfaction, the engineer pried herself loose, insisting she had to check on the ship right away. And while Gill went over the controls with devoted attention, Cherrie dragged the chest the engineer had brought with her into the cockpit. Gill only looked up when Cherrie turned off the receiver, the reporter's nagging voice dying.

"What are they saying now?" she asked warily.

Cherrie waved her hand. "Oh, you know. Some people think we're aliens."

Gill chuckled. "That's nothing new." She went closer and grasped Cherrie's chin, looking her over with knowing eyes.

"What has gotten you upset?"

Cherrie sighed, then she exploded. "They've shown me in that horrible coconaut uniform again!"

Gillian laughed, kissed her pout and laughed some more.

"Ah, sorry cherry pie. But you know I think you look great in anything. Besides, I always kinda liked the name."

Cherrie couldn't help but smile, placated by the ardent adoration in Gill's eyes. She tucked a strand of sweaty hair behind Gill's ear. "Did it go all right? Did you get everything?"

"Hah, they'll never learn. A wig and a Bostonian accent and that's all it took." Gill knelt to open the chest. "I got vegetables from your abuela's garden, the books you wanted, new painting supplies, and ..."

"Coconuts!" Cherrie beamed at the sight of her favorite fruit.

They wandered to their kitchen, Gill helping to chop the vegetables and then contently looking on as Cherrie prepared tamales, singing joyfully at the prospect of fresh food. They sat down in their favorite booth by the diner's window ring, upholstered red leather jumping merrily under their weight as they ravaged their meal, seat-dancing to the groove of Big Mama Thornton's "Hound Dog" blaring from their jukebox. Gill reported on the madness that Roswell had fallen into since their takeoff. When Cherrie kissed the back of her hand, turning her eyes pensively to their far-away home planet, she felt Gill's eyes on her.

"Hey. Are you sure you're still good staying here? So far from your family, from everything?"

Cherrie nodded contently, cradling the hand of her beloved to her cheek.

"Perfectly happy, mi amor. We will come back when our faces aren't on every newspaper and broadcast in the world anymore." She returned her gaze to her partner when she sensed the worry in those blue eyes. "I have everything I want right here. You, the stars, our ship ... and no one trying to take it from us or force us apart."

There was a brief melancholy in Gill's smile at that, but it was fast eclipsed by the tenderness in her gaze when she leaned forward to kiss Cherrie, before looking curiously over her new scrapbook of Earth and finally back to their little blue planet.

"As have I, chérie." She grinned. "And I can't wait to see what you will imagine for Earth."

Roxane Llanque is a German-Bolivian writer, artist, and filmmaker. Her award-winning short film *Aberration* was selected for The Madrid Human Rights Festival and her micro *The Tell-Tale Present* won the 2023 Outstanding Miniature of World Pride Australia. Her writing was featured in the queer horror anthology *Demons & Death Drops*, the sci-fi anthology *We Are All Thieves of Somebody's Future*, and is forthcoming in the Latinx Archive's *Not Your Papi's Utopia: Latinx Visions of Radical Hope*. She is currently working on her first novel. You can find her on social media @roxanellanque.

Wax Mausoleum

by Harper Walton

Lucretia Higginbotham lowers the needle onto the spinning black vinyl disk. Warm, fuzzy crackling seeps out of the gramophone's brass flower, filling her bedroom. The record begins. A compilation of laughter, ranging from low chortles to high-pitched cackles. First, they are separate and distinct, then they overlap to form a cacophony of mirth, like a pack of hyenas have broken into her room. But that would be impossible. Hyenas have long been extinct.

Laughter without a joke preceding it is like a virgin birth, Lucretia thinks. She takes a cigarette from its pack and attaches it to the end of her silver holder. Out the window of her 168th-floor apartment, the lower stories of Flin Flon disappear into smog. Sometimes she wishes her window could be opened, but she understands that they must all be permanently shut to prevent jumping. She turns on the extractor fan to suck away her fumes.

Sitting down at her writing desk, she plugs a wired metal pen into the wall. She lowers its tip directly onto the desk, forming glowing electric letters.

Dear Edith,

I miss you terribly.

I received your electra-postcard from New Bradford this morning. I hope one day I can visit a sky city with you. We will stand at the barrier of one of those infinity viewing platforms, you'll wrap your arms around me from behind, and we'll gaze out across the expanse of air between us and the surface world below. I don't have a technical mind like yours, I have no idea how the tethers hold the city in place. But with you close to me, I wouldn't be scared. You are my tether.

Something rather surprising occurred earlier today, and I must tell you about it in case the news hasn't reached your dirigible yet. I wonder if you're piloting that great inflatable beast as I write these words, or if you've expertly parked it at another metropolis.

There was an enormous fire at Madame Tussauds. It was this morning, so I was out of the building, thank goodness. Can you imagine, the very top of the tallest building in Canada, engulfed in flames? The usual electric beacon beam replaced by a furious orange torch. Thousands of bystanders gathered on platforms nearby to watch. The wax models' sizzling could be heard for miles around. Every time the blaze reached another supply of wax fuel, the inferno would shoot up again through the dome, red and golden, a hundred feet in the air. A friend told me it was a wonderful spectacle, but I'm not sure I would've been able to enjoy it. I would've been too heartbroken for all the artists, who I've met personally, knowing that their many hours of craft and labour have just melted away into nothing. At least they'll still have the molds in their studios so they can remake the figures.

Can you imagine it? Hundreds of firefighters with their bulbous shiny brass helmets, carrying as many wax models out as they can. They were literally melting onto their shoulders! They weren't able to save them all. The fire grew too strong. When I go to work tonight, I'll witness what's left of them. It will be so strange to see my workplace so thoroughly destroyed. Apparently, the dome has completely caved in, leaving only its steel skeleton.

Remember my boss's parrot, Diogenes? Firefighters were able to bring out his cage. He was lying at the bottom of it, motionless, and everyone thought he'd perished. But once he was out in the fresh air, his little red body stirred, and he burst back to life. After a firefighter opened his door he waddled out, said "rotten business!" and flew away.

I must find out who or what caused this fire. Somehow, I don't believe it started itself. But for you, my love, I will be cautious. I can live with losing my workplace, my job, but I can't stand the thought of being taken away from you.

Infinitely yours,
Lucretia

She presses a button at the side of the desk and the words rise off its surface. They travel through her ceiling, and she imagines them joining the gigantic grid of golden thread that covers the entire globe. Lucretia's letter will rush like a streetcar along the electric currents until it finds Edith's portable writing desk in her dirigible's cabin.

Lucretia is proud of her partner, her talented airship pilot, but sometimes the distance between them feels compressed inside her body. The atmospheric pressure is too severe, her skin close to ripping. She imagines herself as a blimp, overinflated with hydrogen, begging to be popped. All she wants, more than anything in the world, is for Edith to materialise at her side and pierce her belly with a sharp needle. But she's on the other side of the planet. Lucretia enjoys receiving electra-postcards, but they're always just a reminder that Edith wishes she was there, not that she actually is. She's been working overtime, taking the extra pay of the night watch, to save up, but how long will it take before she can join Edith on her adventures? Edith doesn't understand, she was born and raised in the upper stories, she went to a penthouse kindergarten, went skiing with her parents on the artificial slopes of New Aspen. Her mother was an airship pilot—it was practically her birthright.

Lucretia looks at the electra-postcards tacked to her peeling bedroom wall. *Greetings from Bath!* She imagines the sprawling metropolis, capital of the Neo-Roman Empire, home to sixty million. *From Amsterdam with love!* Alongside Osaka and Ho Chi Minh City, one of the three great submerged cities Edith has frequented, and Lucretia has only dreamed about. She's used to the heady heights of Flin Flon—she can't imagine what it must be like to explore a place in a submarine, to walk its streets encased in transparent tunnel systems, to eat and drink and sleep in reinforced glass pods, schools of mutated creatures swimming a foot away. Lucretia has never left Flin Flon, let alone Canada.

I mustn't let envy infect our relationship, she thinks, looking at herself sternly in the mirror. *It's not Edith I'm envious of, but the cities which get to spend time with her. I'm jealous of that bloody zeppelin the most! In the last two years, Edith's been inside it much more than she has me.*

Her whole body feels dirty. She takes off her pinstriped pyjamas and climbs into the dry pod in the corner of her small bedroom. She closes the lid. In the dark stainless-steel sphere, she breathes deeply and tries to release the stress and yearning from her body. She prods a button on the inside. A click, then whirring. 42000 hertz of ultrasonic waves pass over her body from every angle, eliminating all bacteria, odours, grime, and unwanted oils. She steps out of the pod warm, reborn.

Back at the dirty mirror, which she can neither afford to replace with a self-cleaning model nor manage to clean often enough herself, she combs her short, sharp bob and applies plum lipstick. Out of habit, she taps the tip of her retroussé nose, smiling because she knows it's Edith's favourite element of her face.

She dresses herself in a flowy white shirt, a dark emerald waistcoat, and her trusty wide-legged palazzo pants. She laces up her leather boots and dons her second-hand brown fur coat. Gloves and a cloche hat complete the ensemble, and she's ready to face the harsh cold of upper-story Flin Flon.

OUTSIDE, SNOW SWIRLS AROUND the thousands of hundred-floored tower blocks that make up Canada's capital. All connected by a network of platforms and steel bridges, the eldest of which shudder in the wind. There's something sweet about their suppleness, the way they are held and swayed by the world's excess energy. *New bridges and buildings are too sturdy*, Lucretia thinks, *too stubborn.* Lucretia stands at the edge of a municipal viewing platform, observing the sea of tall buildings that swallow the horizon. *It's almost unbelievable*, she thinks. *All this used to be rock and muskeg.* She imagines nations walking the land, Inninewak, Metis, Dene. Inuit heading south through Nunvut. She thinks of the thousands of years of local and national history destroyed in the Madame Tussauds fire, the artifacts and relics from Indigenous communities and Flin Flon's industrial past alike, stored in vaults below the wax museum. The fire can't have been an accident. It feels targeted. *But by whom?* Lucretia wonders. *And why? Perhaps the answer lies in the lower levels. It's a good place to start.*

On the way to her district's central elevator, twenty pairs of painted eyes stare back at her. The signs on her local ophthalmologist's. She'd rather go blind than step foot in that godforsaken place.

In the huge elevator, jostling for space with hundreds of other commuters, Lucretia puts on her fluffy earmuffs and flicks a switch on its side. Her favourite song plays. "Laughter Compilation #32," which she listened to daily as a teenager. Back when she was the star center for the Flin Flon Bombers in the major junior hockey league. She misses the rush of gliding on ice towards goal, the power behind every strike, the ripple of the puck hitting the net. As the elevator continues its descent, she remembers her childhood in the lower stories, working shifts at her father's artificial trout-essence factory. Every July, they would work night and day to ensure there was enough supply for the annual trout festival. Her father would tell her how hundreds of years ago, the rivers and lakes were so unpolluted that fish called trout swam in them, and men would snatch them out with curved spikes through their mouths, then cook and eat them. Her mother told her about the beauty contest, in which all the town's young girls would wear skimpy dresses and be judged on their bodies and faces by a committee of men until one was crowned Queen Mermaid.

"Higginbotham Trout Essence Ltd. provides the local community with the most authentic trout taste, based on an old family recipe," her father would say proudly, like he was rehearsing lines for an advert voiceover. "Our ancestors built this city. They worked in zinc refinery—froth flotation and electrowinning plants. And galvanisation. Every piece of iron and steel in Flin Flon is coated in zinc that passed through our forebears' hands. If it wasn't for the Higginbothams, this city would be a corroded, crumbling mess. Never forget that. And what do we get in return? Nothing but an eternity wasting away in the sunless city of the lower levels."

Lucretia wonders if someone like her father, bitter at their lot in life, committed arson against Madame Tussauds, the pinnacle of General Electric Tower, the tallest building in North America. *And if they did,* she thinks, *could you blame them?*

"WHAT'S THE SIX, VAMPS?" Lucretia says to the first teenager she can find.

"No one says vamps anymore, grandma," they reply, only ten or fifteen years younger. "You're clearly not from down here."

"Actually," Lucretia begins, before giving up. "You're right. I was sent down here by Prime Minister Kakanahposquich to investigate the possible arson at Madam Tussauds. Have you heard anything about who might've caused it?"

The teen snorts, flicking a pink fringe out of their androgynous face. "Oh right. Because down here, all of us lowlife scum read *The Sunless City* every night and worship its misogynistic author, and we're always high on datura and prone to violence, so of course one of us took the elevator to the very top of Flin Flon just to destroy the beacon of its history and prosperity, its symbol to the rest of the world of its culture, might, and financial success?"

Lucretia doesn't know what to say to that.

"And then whoever did such a thing had the bravado and stupidity to boast about it to anyone who would listen, and then all it's gonna take is one upper-story big-wig like you to come down here, and we'll spill the beans, and you'll catch the culprit, case closed in time for tea. What is it you lot are eating these days, jellyfish fritters?"

Lucretia is so flustered that she practically runs away from the kid. The melody of their laughter follows her to the end of the block. She won't be able to listen to her favourite record for a while without hearing it. And the worst thing is, she did have jellyfish fritters for dinner last night. What's wrong with her? Has she become something she promised herself she never would? Taken the fancy job at the big institution, in the bell end of the towering phallus of the Canadian government? Paying an arm and a leg for her 168th-floor bedsit, eating fancy takeaway to fill the Edith-shaped hole in her stomach? Buying fancy waistcoats and boots to make herself feel good? Good, or better than who she used to be? Better than the people who she grew up around, who raised her?

The street is covered in grey-black slush, once-pure snow churned by fur-lined arctic boots. Neon signs everywhere for artificial trout essence, second-hand hockey sticks, ice skates, bookshops, pharmacies, porridge parlours. She passes a datura dispensary and is tempted. Her entire life on the straight and narrow. Never once tasting the moonshine her grandfather brewed in a bathtub. How bad could datura be? It's so popular it has a dozen names. Thornapple. Jimsonweed. Devil's trumpet. Hell's bells. One sweet sip would be all she needed. To cleanse her embarrassment, guilt, imposter syndrome. To stop missing Edith. *Does she even miss me? Love me? Is she sleeping with one of the airship's flight attendants?*

Stop.

I need to return to the upper levels or I'll be late for work.

LUCRETIA WAS SURPRISED that work wasn't called off the night after the fire, but her higher ups insisted. "The area is secured," they said, "but we need someone on the ground to make sure no opportunists try to scavenge valuable assets from the rubble. As nightwatchwoman, this may be your most important shift yet."

She was tired of playing detective. Maybe it was arson as an act of class warfare. Maybe it was a sexist or racist statement against Prime Minister Alsoomse Kakanahposquich. Her un-breathing doppelganger now an effigy, melted into the floor of the monument to her continued success.

Forget wax museum, she thinks, *now it's a wax mausoleum*. She imagines Geraldine Clarke, mayor of Flin Flon, descendant of local legend Bobby Clarke, inducted into the Hockey Hall of Fame for his triumphs with the Philadelphia Flyers. Melted. Tom Creighton, the prospector who found the minerals that led Flin Flon to formation. Disfigured. J.E. Preston Muddock, the author who wrote the dime store novel *The Sunless City* in 1905, whose main character gave the town its name. Dripping. And Flin Flon himself, Josiah Flintabbaty Flonatin, the fictional prospector and explorer, addicted to snuff—a wax model of a man who never existed, but whose abbreviated name now lives on in the capital of Canada and one of the largest cities in the world, congealing in a puddle, surrounded by ash.

Lucretia finds it funny how outdated the 1020-year-old book is. In it, Josiah buys a submarine and explores a seemingly bottomless lake in the Rocky Mountains. He ventures deeper and deeper until he passes through into a city in which everything is backwards to him—the local currency is tin, some people have tails, and the government is a council of women. Flintabbaty Flonatin doesn't like this, so he escapes through an extinct volcano.

Josiah would've hated today's society, Lucretia thinks. Most world leaders are women, whilst men tend to take up positions in manual labour in the lower stories of cities. It's not hard to understand why many men see the author, Preston Muddock, as a prophet, who predicted men's reversal of fortune. Lucretia has heard of groups being formed who sanctify *The Sunless City* like a bible.

For many, Flin Flon is a city named after a man, founded by a man, and built by men's labour. It was founded in 1927 by Hudson Bay Mining and Smelting to exploit the large local copper and zinc ore resources. It used to be on the border of Manitoba and Saskatchewan, but now it's so big it's become its own province. If the Madame Tussauds fire was indeed arson, Lucretia's money is on a lower-story man inspired by the city's namesake.

BACK UP IN FLIN FLON'S HEIGHTS, Lucretia enjoys the thin, fresh air. The snow is still falling, turning the whole city white and grey. She walks past a window and peers into a stranger's apartment. The woman inside is jogging on a vintage treadmill made from a tank's caterpillar tracks, watching a film projected onto a giant pearlescent oyster shell. As a teenager, Lucretia would have laughed at people like this. Now, envy curls itself around her ribcage.

For a moment, she wonders if the Madame Tussauds fire might have been a personal attack. Perhaps someone she hurt on an ice rink when playing for the Bombers? Someone from her English class in school who she accidentally embarrassed by correcting? A bitter former lover? Impossible, she was single and lonely her entire life before meeting Edith. *Is that why I'm so scared to lose her?* Lucretia wonders. *I can't go back to how things were.*

No, she definitely wasn't the target. Anyone who would've done the tiniest bit of research would know that she only works nocturnally and would have planned the arson for night-time. In the end, the fire only caused property damage. Everyone was able to evacuate in time. If the arsonist had murderous intentions, they well and truly failed.

LUCRETIA ARRIVES AT THE PLATFORM outside the 216th floor of General Electric Tower. She almost gasps. Her workplace, where she spends most of her time outside of her apartment, reduced to a giant rusty birdcage.

Night has fallen. She takes the internal elevator to the tower's top floor.

"Hey, Wuttunee," she says, smiling to the watchman she's about to replace.

"Electra-letter came through for you," he says, passing her a portable writing desk.

It trembles slightly in Lucretia's fingers.

Dear Lucretia,

My co-pilot has taken the wheel and we are cruising at an al-titude of 14,000 feet. I couldn't wait until the end of my shift to write this letter. Hearing of the fire at Madame Tussauds terrified me. What if it had been merely a few hours earlier, when you were still working? What if you'd been trapped under a fallen beam and were roasted alive? The thought of it made me sick, made me cry. I simply can't lose you. I am so lonely, living in the sky, going from city to city. So what if they're beautiful and fascinating? They mean nothing if I can't witness them with you.

I've decided to cut my tour short and will return to Flin Flon at the next available opportunity. Once I'm back, I'd like you to take a sabbatical and travel the world with me. If you still haven't saved up enough, I'll cover the rest. It's time you had the adventure you've always deserved.

I'm sorry I've been distant, geographically and emotionally. I'm sorry I sometimes make ignorant comments about your upbringing—I'm trying to unlearn a lot of harmful stereotypes about people from the lower stories that were drilled into me from an early age. I'm sorry I don't tell you enough how amazing you are and how beautiful I find you (especially your nose) and how I love the clothes you wear and those laughter records you listen to.

I love you, Lucretia. And I can't wait to love you in a dozen more cities around the world.

Yours and no one else's,
Edith

"You alright?" Wuttunee asks.

Lucretia nods, wiping a tear from her eye. She nods again, can't stop nodding.

"Have a good shift."

"Can't go any worse than this morning," she laughs.

She deposits her things in a locker and changes into a navy boilersuit. It should all feel familiar, but this is no ordinary shift. She is fine working nights because she grew up in the lower levels, where tall buildings block out any sunlight. Usually, she passes the time walking around the exhibitions, learning about Flin Flon history, Canadian history, and First Nations history, and chatting unreciprocated with the wax models. She's aware that most people would find a dark empty wax museum disturbing, but she is comfortable around the lifeless figures. She wouldn't admit this to anyone, except maybe Edith, but they're the closest things she has to friends. She kills time reading books, daydreaming about Edith, eating pickled carrot sandwiches, and practising different types of laughter.

But now, everything is different. Through the exposed roof, snowflakes flutter down, landing on deformed faces and arms. Dismembered limbs and severed heads lie on the floor where they were left to roll. Glass eyes swivelling back into concave sockets. Wigs burned like cotton candy onto greasy scalps. The models that could not be saved. Lucretia spots the prime minister kneeling—or made to kneel by her molten kneecaps. Mayor Geraldine Clarke has fallen to her side and fused with her hockey-playing ancestor, Bobby. Tom Creighton, Preston Muddock, and Flin Flon himself, the three founding fathers of the city, flaccid, droopy, liquified then resolidified into forms they were never supposed to take. *If anyone set fire to this place to make a statement*, Lucretia thinks, *it got lost in translation*.

Lucretia wonders why she even wants to solve the mystery. To prove she's good at her job? To get a promotion? Because she's naturally curious and it's fun to play detective? To distract herself from missing Edith?

A clear "ding" rings out from the portable writing desk. A message from her boss.

Please check the Chamber of Horrors. Somehow, it was the only room that survived unscathed. Probably the reinforced door.

Lucretia enters the code and steps into the complete black. She reaches for the light switch, but when she flicks it, nothing happens. She checks the fuse box, but it isn't blown. Probably some fire damage to the whole electric system. She takes a flashlight from her duffel bag and enters the Chamber of Horrors once more. She hates these flashlights with their zinc-carbon batteries. They require rest at short intervals, so they only provide temporary bursts of light. It's not that no one's invented anything better, it's that her boss is so stingy he doesn't want to cough up for new gear. Lucretia's been telling him for ages about a product, a portable baton-shaped bulb with a circular base that you can stick on any surface and activate by lifting like a lever. Edith told her about them in a letter, saying she uses them on the dirigible.

As if on cue, the flashlight dies for good. Lucretia digs around in the supply closet for a last resort. Candles. Poetic, really, wax allowing her to see more of itself.

She cautiously pads into the Chamber of Horrors. The flame flickers in front of her. She never steps foot in this room un-less she absolutely has to, and always with every available light switched on. Her body is a cocktail glass full of fear and giddy thoughts of Edith. The orange glow gets caught on dozens of faces—all criminals, tyrants, dictators—leering at her. A room full of men at the top of the world. Adolf Hitler, Vlad the Im-paler, Genghis Khan, serial killers, necrophiliacs. Lucretia stands in the middle of the room, surrounded. The men stare at her like judges at a Flin Flon beauty contest hundreds of years ago. Except she's the only one in the running so she's automatically crowned Queen Mermaid, but the men are still there, unblink-ing, smiling without moving their lips. Lucretia is frozen to the spot. She forgets who she is, where she is, what year it is, what she's doing.

Lucretia drops the candle. A wax body erupts in flames. The candle rolls on the carpet, setting it alight. The room is engulfed in orange waves, glowing golden feathers licking every surface. *It's beautiful,* Lucretia thinks. She can't wait to tell Edith about it. Lucretia rushes out and slams the door behind her. She grabs a telephone and dials the emergency number. The fire brigade is on its way. She runs down the stairs to the nearest platform. How will she explain this to her boss? Maybe like the first fire, it will remain forever unexplained. Maybe that too was an accident. She doesn't care anymore. She's quitting anyway. She's quitting. She's smiling. She's running back to her apartment, back to her cleaning pod, back to her laughter records, back to her wardrobe full of nice clothes, back to her soft bed, back to herself, back to waiting for Edith, who's coming soon, her love, back so soon she's practically there already.

Harper Walton is the editor of the short story anthology *Carnival at the End of the World* (Buoy Press). They've received Highly Commended in the Manchester Cathedral poetry prize and Creative Future writers' awards, achieved Third Place in the Brick Lane Bookshop short story prize, and won two Young Poets Network challenges.

The Transdimensional Adventure of an Aviatrix

by Antoinette Rydyr

One million years ago a caveman earnestly chipped away at a boulder. A woman dressed in jodhpurs and a leather flying jacket entered the cave.

"Thag, look after Baby, I have exploring to do."

The brutish Paleolithic man remained focussed on his task.

"Thag!" the woman insisted, tapping his hairy shoulder. "Look after Baby." On the ground was spread an animal pelt peppered with holes, and she laid Baby upon the soft fur.

"Goo," Baby gurgled.

Thag looked up. "Mela go out again?"

"Yes, Mela go out. I must find the door that links our times."

35

"Much danger. Thag save Mela from cannibals."

"Yes, you did, sweetheart."

"Thag save Mela from giant bird."

"Thank you, Thag, but it wasn't a bird. It was an airplane, and one day I shall fly us away from here."

MELA EXITED THE CAVE, and Thag returned to his work. Although Thag's concentration was intense, it was not enough to block out the odour. Fowl vapours emanated from Baby.

"Goo," Baby gurgled.

Thag grunted.

He picked up Baby, took it to the river, removed its banana-leaf nappy, and washed Baby. When Baby was clean and dry, he wrapped a fresh banana-leaf around Baby's bottom and secured it with a hooked bone, which he designed himself.

He returned to the cave, placed Baby down on the fur skin, and continued chipping at the rock.

LATER, MELA RETURNED, threw down a dead sabretooth she'd snared while exploring.

"I caught us some dinner, Thag."

Thag inspected the fresh carcass. Frowned. He poked his finger at multiple holes ruining the pelt.

"I'm sorry, dear, but my tommy-gun is an automatic. I promise to modify it to single-shot."

A STRANGE BEING ENTERED the cave. "Amelia Earhart, I presume."

"And you are?"

"I am B'zytl, from one million years in your future."

Mela studied the humanoid. He had a large dome head and six fingers on each hand.

"You look unexpectedly different."

"We have evolved. We have infinite intelligence and greater dexterity."

"I see. How did you find me?"

"By applying quantum mechanics to block-universe theory in which everything past, present, and future exists simultaneously. It enabled me to travel through space-time. I just had to find the right door."

"Gracious! You've found the door! I've been looking everywhere for it."

In an exaggerated gesture of imploration, B'zytl dropped to one knee and held out his clasped hands. "Come to the future, Amelia. Your pioneer legend will be celebrated."

Mela hid a titter of amusement behind her hand. The scene was reminiscent of a vaudeville show she had once attended. But her momentary glee faded as she caught sight of Thag diligently chipping the stone.

"But what of Thag?"

B'zytl stood, straightened to full height, and puffed out his chest. "He's just a primitive. Leave him." He added punctuation with a flourish of his six-fingered hand.

"No. Thag is an inventor. He's very single-minded, thorough, and steadfast in his objective." She leaned in, whispered, "He's inventing the wheel, you know. Any day now..." Mela beamed proudly.

B'zytl frowned.

"I've always been attracted to intellectuals," she assured him. "And there's Baby to consider."

"Goo," Baby gurgled.

Mela smiled warmly at Baby, then returned her attention to the futuristic visitor. "We can all go to the future together," she exclaimed.

"No, only you, Amelia. The item specifications are calibrated to your DNA, garnered from a single follicle retrieved from your hairbrush. It took twenty years of red tape and bypassed protocols to be granted permission for a single unit to travel against the tide of time. For an entire entourage to travel would take a century of hurdle-jumping and hoop-diving."

Deflated, Mela pondered for a moment. She paced the cave, tapping her finger on her chin while in deep contemplation. Then a lightbulb switched on.

"But if time is relative, you can start the process now, jump to the future to attain permission, then jump straight back to this time again," Mela declared profoundly.

B'zytl frowned again as he tried to jimmy fault into her logic. His heart sank. This was not the plan at all. His glory and amorous pursuits were being scuttled by this infernal woman and her propensity for brilliance. Could she not recognise his grand intellect? His desired objective and subjective desire were slipping from his grasp in favour of a brute and a baby.

B'zytl released a deep sigh. "I shall consult the mathematicians to see if there is a solution to the dilemma." As a quick afterthought, B'zytl added a forced grin hoping to mask the falsehood.

"Please do." Mela placed a hand on B'zytl's shoulder. And squeezed. He felt his legs waver along with his resolve.

"I shall await your return, B'zytl. Shall we say in a couple of weeks? You know, to allow time for Thag to finish his project." She gave a disarming wink, and this time his resolve weakened by a zettametre.

"Very well, I will do my best," B'zytl conceded.

An unpleasant aroma rose from Baby's leaf-diaper.

His olfactory senses assaulted, B'zytl screwed up his nose. He stuffed a piece of paper into Mela's hand before beating a hasty departure. "I must go now but will leave the door open a crack in case you change your mind."

Mela studied the note covered in mathematical symbols directing her to the time portal.

"Don't forget to take a sample of hair from Thag and Baby," Mela called, but he had already left.

Certain of B'zytl's infatuation for her, Mela smiled knowingly. "He'll be back," she thought to herself as she pocketed the note.

MELA COUNTED HER BLESSINGS as she surveyed her surroundings. A loving, protective mate. A bundle of joy cooing merrily. A warm, safe home inside the cave, and wild adventures outside. Mela smiled at Thag, gave him a tender peck on his sloping forehead as he stoically continued his work. Although out of time, she did not feel out of place and would not change anything for the world.

"Not one thing," Mela ruminated contentedly.

An odour wafted up from Baby and punched her in the nose, snapping her out of her reverie.

"Goo," Baby gurgled.

She picked up Baby and held the infant at arm's length. "Maybe one thing."

Antoinette Rydyr is an artist/writer working in the genres of science-fiction, fantasy, and horror usually bent into a surrealist and satirical angle. Using the acronym SCAR, she works with fellow creator Steve Carter and together they have produced graphic novels, award-winning screenplays, and esoteric electronic music. In 2023 they were awarded the Ledger of Honour by the Comics Arts Awards of Australia.

Antoinette's stories include: "Mother Dandelion," an Aurealis Award finalist published in *Spawn: Weird Horror Tales About Pregnancy, Birth and Babies*; "Every Part of Her," published in *Killer Creatures Down Under: Horror Stories with Bite*; and her collaborative steampunk western novels, *Weird Wild West,* were published by Bizarro Pulp Press, USA.

SCAR have also published several graphic novels which can be found on their website along with other surrealist art: www.weirdwildart.com.

The Match for This Century and All the Centuries to Come

by Anthony Boulanger

If only one word could be used to describe Reykjavík on the tenth of July 1972, it would have to be 'electric.' It applied as much to the weather as to the mood. Passersby's hair stood on end as soon as a zeppelin docked with a Tesla-Eiffel tower to recharge—one of those trademarked gigantic towers for embarking and disembarking passengers—and the few pubs were packed to the rafters with comments and expectations.

Around the Laugardalshöll hall and the two champions' hotels, it was impossible to get around by car because of police restrictions, and very difficult on foot because of the density of journalists and onlookers hoping to catch a movement behind a window, a surreptitious image of Bobby Fischer and his team on one side of town, or Boris Spassky and his comrades on the other.

Large cathode-ray screens were being installed in the main thoroughfares for all those eager to follow the chess matches live, and huge Edison-Tesla Inc. relay towers were undergoing final tests to relay what everyone was calling the *Match of the Century* all over the world and as far as the neutral space station orbiting 408 kilometers above the volcanic island. On paper, it was the 1972 World Chess Championship, but no one on the planet was fooled by the fact when what was actually at stake, symbolically and materially, was world domination of one bloc over another.

Whoever won the war on the sixty-four squares would win the world.

A few flashbulbs went off in anticipation as a resident of the American hotel exited the lobby. Many others followed as journalists recognized Isaac Asimov himself—the last surviving member of the legendary robotics trio—by his walk and haircut. The biochemist and writer gave a debonair wave, a few words about the Russian, the reigning champion, and merely smiled when asked about the American challenger. As a binational, and despite the relative period of détente between the two blocs, Asimov was one of the few diplomatic and scientific bridges between the titans who were about to clash. Without pressing the pace, Asimov took the direction of Laugardalshöll hall. Once he had crossed the security cordon, he waited patiently, book in hand.

A murmur spread through the nearby ranks of journalists as an acacia wood cockpit topped by three balloons appeared, piercing the cloudy ceiling and heading towards the Tesla-Eiffel tower to tie up. The symbols on the balloons were instantly recognizable: the Government of the United African Nations was inviting itself to the event, and it was a safe bet that Cheikh Anta Diop, Senegalese by birth and a regular representative of the African continent, was on board. His presence alone was likely to remind the diplomats and politicians present that when two blocs were mentioned in the Cold War that was about to be settled today, it was only because four other continents were left out.

"They say Carl Sagan has just arrived by boat," someone murmured.

The murmur soon turned into a tidal wave, amplified when news of the presence of the nuclear physicist Hélène Langevin-Joliot reached the crowd. Soon everyone was adding to the story, and when it became clear that neither Team Fischer nor Team Spassky would show up or comment, journalists were quick to fall back on passenger manifests from zeppelins, ornithopters, and ocean-going vessels. Reykjavík suddenly took on a new dimension as an exceptional density of scientists from so many disciplines gathered in the same place at the same time. For a moment, the presence of the world's best chess players was eclipsed by the Nobel Prize and Fields Medal winners who had arrived via the Asian Empire's hydrotrain system: Richard Feynman, Tomonaga Shin'ichirō, Yang Chen-Ning, Dorothy Hodgkin, Ulf von Euler, Laurent Schwartz, and many others.

When night fell on the Icelandic capital, no one had managed to extract a single comment from any of its illustrious names, and no one knew when in the history of mankind such an excess of intellect had been brought together in one place.

IT WAS NINE O'CLOCK when the spectators who had been lucky enough to get a ticket to sit in the Laugardalshöll were finally able to enter. Bleachers sat on either side of the hall, framing a single chessboard and its clock. The chairs in front of both the white and black pieces were off-center.

It was 9:30 a.m. when the hubbub with the growing crowds naturally died down as Carl Sagan appeared in front of the stands. He waved, almost absent-mindedly, as the first applause broke out. Someone handed a microphone to the eminent astronomer, and he allowed the silence to settle for a few seconds.

"Ladies and gentlemen," began the professor, "I'd like to welcome you to Reykjavík for this World Chess Championship. I've been asked, rather impromptu, to say a few words to you before the two players enter because of the exceptional nature of the match. I don't think the organizing committee has in mind the same characteristics to define this moment as I do."

Sagan paused and glanced towards the corridors where each team was waiting.

"It is true that you are going to see an American trying to put an end to the Soviet hegemony that has lasted since 1948. But for my part, I am delighted that a very large number of colleagues from all continents have been able to join us in Iceland, because the physical and chemical sciences community has decided, at the invitation of Dr. Asimov, to organize an exceptional Solvay Conference, which will begin tomorrow. I would have liked to give the floor to Isaac, but he had a last-minute adjustment to make with the Russian team," Sagan explained.

"This is the deal we have in mind, and the one on the basis of which we sent out all our invitations: all the scientists present agree to put themselves at the service of the Union—the United States or the Soviet Union—that becomes the world champion. We are just one Earth, one species. These wars and political games are preventing our planet from being anything more than a blue dot in its galaxy. We scientists have a duty to take our rightful place to ensure a viable, sustainable, and ultimately space-faring life for all future generations."

Sagan put the microphone down on the table, indifferent to the slight clatter that came from the loudspeakers. He nodded to a few spectators, and a thunderous applause broke out in the room, which grew louder when Bobby Fischer appeared from a cloakroom. But the applause was short-lived. Behind the

American champion came Boris Spassky, but all eyes rapidly focused on the two silhouettes towering over the players.

Two metal humanoids moved cautiously forward. TTA machines… designed by Turing, animated by Tesla, then educated by Asimov. Although robots had been around since the 1920s, it was not until 1939 that they reached a level of autonomy and complexity that enabled them to take action on the fronts of the Second World War. Since then, automatons had been relegated to work in the fields and mines.

The American robot had a sharply angled face covered in a thin film of silver and a lanky body of the same shade. It towered over the tall Fischer and the rest of the humans by two heads. The Russian robot, adorned in red and gold, appeared more compact, preferring roundness to the edges of the American.

The robots took their places in front of the chessboard. Fischer and Spassky took their places on the chairs.

Bobby Fischer turned towards the nearest spectators. "The robots will dictate the moves, which we will reproduce on the chessboard, filmed from above and displayed on the screens. For the record, neither Mr. Spassky nor I have ever beaten our artificial equivalent."

Boris Spassky nodded soberly at these words.

"This year's championship will be played over twenty-four games," he concluded.

THE FIRST PART BEGAN a few moments later. It lasted more than three hundred moves. Some seemed aberrant, only to be explained much later, when a pawn was captured or bishops exchanged. Opportunities for capture turned out to be traps. The experts recognized them as such after the event. The two robots faced each other in a terrible silence, punctuated only by the clicking of the dials displaying the moves and the light shock of the pieces the humans picked up and placed down. The game was declared a draw by the two machines when only the kings were left on the board.

In the second bout, the game was shorter. Two hundred and sixty-nine moves. Another draw.

While the following games were just as interesting in terms of the moves made by the two inhuman intelligences, they were just as unsatisfying in terms of the score. From draw to stalemate, the robots never seemed to be able to gain the upper hand over each other, and as the temperature in the great hall rose, so did the tension. Someone in the audience called out to Asimov, who had worked on the two machines and was the last survivor of the Turing-Tesla-Asimov triad, but the Russian American just shrugged. He had taught these robots to play chess, and on this eleventh of July 1972, they were taking the game to levels of complexity no human had ever approached before.

In the twenty-fourth game the American robot had white, but he didn't start the game. He raised his parallelepiped head towards his metal brother and asked for a draw. The Russian machine agreed. The world championship ended without a winner. *Or were there two?* wondered the organizers and referees. In the event of a tie, shouldn't the title go to the outgoing champion? This time it was the Russian robot who intervened. In his choppy, mechanical voice, he interrupted the discussions.

"You don't understand, this situation is perfectly and mathematically normal and logical. Neither the United States nor the Soviet Union won. The TTA Machines did. Neither Bobby Fischer nor Boris Spassky could beat us. We couldn't break the tie. So, we declare the machine superior to the human, and my brother and I take over the reins of this world."

"In agreement with this," added the American robot, "and sharing Professor Sagan's vision, we will welcome the ideas of the scientists who put themselves at our service. We will not replace them. We robots have a duty to take our place to ensure you a viable, sustainable, and ultimately space-faring life for all future generations. We will be leading the Solvay Congress tomorrow. You will come to the conclusion that this is the best possible way forward. Thank you for your attention."

The two robots withdrew, leaving Laugardalshöll in a silence of stunned indecision.

"Damn it," muttered Sagan to himself. "Isaac, it's happening just as you predicted in your invitation. If I hadn't been here to see it …"

"Predicted? I've programmed it!" replied the biochemist. "The next step is for them to program themselves! Look at what they've done with chess, imagine what they'll do when they can modify themselves!"

"Gods …" someone breathed behind the backs of the two scientists.

Originally from the Rouen area, France, **Anthony Boulanger** now lives in the Norman countryside, in the company of his muse and their three children.

He works on short stories as well as novels and scripts for role-playing games and comics. His favourite subjects are birds, golems, and world mythologies.

The Battle
for Girola

by Angela Acosta

*D**roopy planets wilt under the siege of bombs, and the far-thest stars buckle under the pressure*, the Bard of War wrote.

"Ah, if only I had my sketchbook to trace the paths these bombs are making across the sky. It's quite surreal, as if the fighters were conjuring shooting stars. That's a lovely metaphor. Perhaps my assistant will help me with the next draft," they muttered to themself, twirling the stylus contentedly in their fingers.

Explosions hit the atmosphere of Girola, smudging like brilliant gold and violet oil pastels. A telescope they had installed for this very purpose granted them almost unlimited access to a horizon overcome by starship scrimmages and the bombs the gunners volleyed towards the surface of the planet. This far away, the people on the ground were mere smudges on a tapestry of galactic proportions.

The ship rocked, shaking to and fro as the cloaking device worked to keep the Bard of War perched safely away from the worst of the action. They had to record every moment faithfully, a photorealistic representation at the behest of rich benefactors. Once their crew stabilized the craft, they continued composing their epic. What was once a job had become an obsession. Their nimble fingers twitched whenever not touching a stylus or console, strumming up more and more stanzas.

"Verdant continents of towered citadels
float along a primordial sea of people:
warriors, scholars, seers, and playwrights.
Whether through telescopes or human optics,
they witness a kaleidoscopic sky,
bracing for the impact of falling debris.

Girola holds steady against the battering ram,
its bravest warriors adorned in iron of old,
coordinating the offense with silicon microchips.
Girola never capitulates, aiming for a new zenith,
a new era as the Traval dynasty takes power
and grants her darling planet life anew."

The Bard of War was satisfied, even humbled, by their latest creation. These epic poems they so dutifully crafted were renowned throughout human inhabited space. Each time they were invited to watch a firefight, they jetted off to the far reaches of a warzone. Their writing fingers quivered not from the thrust of the shuttle launch but in anticipation of a new battle, a new spark of poetic inspiration. A still-life painting could not suffice for the momentous power of these stellar dramas carried out by humans and androids. The Bard's dendrites lit up watching the explosions on Girola, and they begged to get closer. This was going to be better than any holo vid.

They heard their crew make the requisite verbal exchanges to land, but such formalities were mere background noise. At the right tempo, words turned into the beat of generations for the Bard of War's synesthetic pleasure. Once their ship received clearance to land from the Traval dynasty, the pilots guided the craft close to one of the poles before cruising at ten kilometers above the scorched planet to their targeted landing site. Although the Bard of War was strapped within the confines of a safety harness, they continued devising sonnets, villanelles, and odes in their mind, poems fit for the Traval ruler who would soon reign over Girola. Their brain hummed in satisfaction, quieting the parts of themself that never shut off, winding gears loaded with the antiseptic sting of a past where the cold prose of childhood was all they knew. They should take their medicine soon.

While the crew was handling the landing procedures, they offloaded their memories of the firefight onto the ship's computer. These poems would one day grace the royal halls in the capital city they were once exiled from. Everyone would recognize them as a true bard, the flâneuse of the Traval dynasty, unsullied by the fear and shame that had brought them to this moment. They would become a genderless myth, the spirit of the age, a zeitgeist that would set whole star systems ablaze in resplendent brilliance.

The last battle lay heavy on their mind, sifting through the sieve of the hexadecimal verse in their memory retrieval software.

"Bombs christen new ground as the shock troops clear the land, the Battle of Atlanta, named for the heroine Atalanta and General Sherman, from the war-torn Terra from whence we came, a colony united will soon be won."

They thought gleefully about what rhymes and caesura would come out of this battle, that is until they were rudely, but necessarily, interrupted by the task at hand. Boots on the ground, fresh poetic meter trailing after survey equipment.

"Mark your verse, Bard," the defence squad leader instructed. "I implore you to exercise extreme caution. I am limiting your exposure to planetary atmosphere to three hours. You are at risk of nuclear radiation, so do not remove your face shield and maintain awareness of the Geiger counter. My troops will follow behind you."

"Relax, at least this planet has hearty gravity, a full one-and-a-half g. My assistant will stay onboard while I chart a course for the ruins about a kilometer east. I sense there may be some survivors I can interview," they responded with the nonchalance of someone who had long stopped taking an interest in their own mortality.

Gravity threatened to swallow them whole. They were used to tumbling across moons and asteroids, but this planet was laden with a gravity well as thick as hot desert battlefields. It felt wrong, like parts of them had been jumbled together and they were suddenly all too aware of existing in a body of flesh and bone. Maybe they'd ask to upgrade to a mech that would provide a proper exosuit.

Trying not to think too hard about the civilian casualties, the Bard of War stepped over rubble that once held sentients' dreams. There would be ruin, there would be remains. There may very well be found poems within the rubble. They almost wished their once-parents could see how brave they were being as they served a greater purpose for the Traval dynasty.

A voice, a witness. Oh, the muses would be quite satisfied.

"Why are you here?" a survivor cried, recognizing the gold insignia on the Bard of War's suit.

Ever the consummate professional, they took out their microphone and asked, "Ma'am, could you tell me what happened here?" Visions of calvary and cannons of old mixed with images of buildings pockmarked with damage from lasers and blasters.

"What does it look like?" she spat back.

"Ma'am, I'm just doing my job."

"This was my life! Can't you see that? And now all that will remain of me is whatever nonsensical drivel you decide to write about Girola. My name is Berenice, with three e's, would you at least do me the decency of remembering that?" She exaggerated the pronunciation of her first name that came from a language known on Terra as Spanish.

"Oh, but of course." They smiled, listening to the constant click of the Geiger counter, a metronome for their poetry.

Thinking quickly, she demanded, "Give me your digital notebook."

"Why? I haven't even begun writing in this one yet."

"Give it to me, now!"

"Is that a threat?"

"What's the worst I could do anyway, write something? What authority do you have if you probably have no inkling what 'Girola' even means? Girola, turning planet, the one habitable sphere in this system."

Annoyed, the Bard dropped the notebook, and took a step back. Berenice urged herself into an awkward seated position on the ground. She took the stylus and began writing.

Though her letters were small and hurried, she read aloud once her work was done.

"The Bard of War has visited me,
a woman wrought by rolling earthquakes
and the din of heartache.
I fear it means this war has taken me.

Neither hostage nor soldier was I,
and like a poet I shall die.
May this planet one day see sovereignty.
Berenice, solar year 2543."

They were impressed. This human woman had a way with verse.

She held the notebook up to activate the facial recognition software then hit "Publish" on the message she had just composed. Before the Bard knew what had happened, she had thrust the notebook back into their gloved hands.

"Wait, what did you just—" the Bard cried out.

The notebook glowed as the view count began increasing exponentially. The Bard would have to answer to a superior about this misstep.

"Who are you?" the Bard asked.

"What does it look like? I'm one of the Bards of Girola. I am a story keeper, not that the dozens of ships up there would care."

"A … story keeper?" How had they never heard of such a thing?

"Are you that daft? Of course there are poets on planets too, not just the ones the Traval dynasty appoints. A story keeper tells of the lives and deeds of her people. She learns the coastline of her planet, conferring with fellow story keepers wherever she travels. She remembers each sentient being that has lost their life because of these endless wars. Now, I suppose I should thank you for giving me the dignity of writing my own obituary." She gave the Bard a slight bow.

The Bard of War was angry, but a weird mixture of astonishment and horror soon took over. Nobody had ever written back to them like that, extending a few lines across the void of space, or heavy planetary gravity in this case. She was much more fortunate and fulfilled than they ever were. All they did was run from their past, relishing in anonymity. She could be an asset, this Berenice.

"Come with me, you could be of great use to—"

"No, me digas tonterías, *poet!* Don't give me that nonsense. This is the only planet I've known. You and I are nothing alike. I already told you to leave me alone. Let me nurse the wounds of my fallen comrades while I still can."

"That language, those words you just used, I thought they were…" They couldn't quite say 'extinct.'

"Oh, now you're all smitten by my exotic language!"

One of the defense squad members interrupted, "Bard, there's a new report about two kilometers south of here, we need to go!"

"Go, and don't come back. You never were welcome here among my people anyway," Berenice retorted.

The defense squad was already on the move, and without another word, the Bard of War turned and left. They were safe, they would stay safe in this gig and body.

From the ruins on Girola to the path their ship took to leave the star system, Berenice's voice echoed in their mind. The words she wrote haunted the inhabited star systems like a digital ghost in the machine. They were loath to admit just how much each stanza, dutifully timestamped at 14:00 every week, roused the Bard of War to respond in turn. Such automated messages said little about her continued survival, though perhaps this story keeper made it off world after all. This week, Berenice sent them a single stanza.

> "I send our stories skyward, if only to give credence
> to these wounds that mark skin and metal in equal measure.
> I write for my siblings who dream of faraway stations,
> for my elders toiling and singing songs of old,
> and for ancestors on sunbaked plains and mountain steppes."

If the Bard's voice and verse could propagate through space, then they would make sure Berenice's messages would travel all the way to the Traval controlled senate. The Bard of War had sacrificed their identity for their profession, an exosuit protecting them from abuse and misunderstanding. Berenice had done

what they never could, and maybe, just maybe, they could both
lend a few verses to ending this perpetual war.

"Humans program and command galleons and rocket ships,
shouting orders in steam-pressed garments with insignias.
For years, these soldiers offered me collegiality,
ensuring safe passage in exchange for poetry.

I shed my name and origin story for a taste
of divine righteousness and allegiance
while droopy planets morphed into grotesque
spheres of Traval influence.

Girola sang back to me, a verse so untamed
and beautifully harmonic I cried out in her
found poetry, caressing gullies formed by lasers,
breathing out healing to a curse
I let pass through my lips, too."

The Bard of War, solar year 2543.

Angela Acosta (she/her) is a bilingual Mexican American
writer who holds a Ph.D. in Iberian Studies from The Ohio
State University. She is an Assistant Professor of Spanish
at the University of South Carolina. She is a 2022 Dream
Foundry Contest for Emerging Writers Finalist, 2022 Somos
en Escrito Extra-Fiction Contest Honorable Mention, and
Rhysling finalist. Her writing has appeared in *Copihue Poetry*,
Shoreline of Infinity, *Apparition Lit*, *Radon Journal*, and *Space
& Time*. She is author of *Summoning Space Travelers* (Hiraeth
Publishing, 2022) and *A Belief in Cosmic Dailiness: Poems of a
Fabled Universe* (Red Ogre Review, 2023).

Coketown, Mars

by Gregory Lawrence

I'm at the counter of a cheap-looking corner shop in the Night-All-Day district, picking up a six-pack of own-brand coke to unwind after work, when something flashes in the top right corner of my field of vision. A message from Witsel, my contact in a mining corp.

Urgent drone retirement job at Liberty Mining & Services Compound 6. Expedited rate doubled.

I nod, and my intent to accept the job is eye-scanned. Likewise, my intent to pay for that six-pack before I've even seen the price. 429 credits!

"That can't be right," I mutter.

A drone in an old-style spacesuit shoots up from behind the counter. No use arguing with drones—they're just electronics in a suit. Then the opaque visor opens, revealing a very human, toothy grin. Suits like these either make people look like drones, or remind me of those ancient photos of the first man on Mars or Earth's moon. Still better to wear an old suit than no suit here, just in case the oxygen supply fails.

"Sorry," the man says, not the least bit apologetic. "Sales are final."

Sometimes I feel like I'm the only one in Coketown, Mars, who still makes an honest living. The guy's got a UD badge on his chest. Universal Debit worker. No wonder he can't afford a nude-suit like mine. He doesn't make what you could call a living, even if he was one of the honest ones, still paying off his UD balance from the journey from Earth or whatever stupid choices he made here. The drones, of course, don't quite make a living either, since they're not alive.

I step out into the Pleasure Palisades. Hopefully the six-pack will be enough for the night job—the cheap, synthetic cocaine in own-brand sodas wears off a bit quickly. To be honest, though, I prefer the job over going home to my son. We'd probably argue. Guelph is eighteen, an adult now but not acting it. Not pulling his weight, neither at home nor in the family business. I shoot him a message that he'll be in charge of any urgent business calls.

I get a response straight away. But no, it's another message from Liberty Mining & Services.

Drone LMS-D1#0912nTv2 will pick you up in a black rover-craft in 3 minutes.

So they sent a drone to get me. I don't mind much. Guelph, of course, would mind, though he wouldn't say so, not unless he's with that awful luddite old-schooler crowd he's been hanging with.

I walk to my pick-up location at the district's entrance gate, sipping on a can. Recently, most of my career counsellor work has been retiring drones. Not that I'm complaining. It's easier work, decommissioning machines. The corporations used to do it themselves, but they've outsourced the job to private contractors like me since the Human/Drone Acts.

There's the rovercraft. The drone makes quick work of the distance across the orange dustscape, the Sinosphere dome looming large over everything with its outer shell painted luminous blues and greens. That undertaking has surely missed its mark. Instead of evoking second-hand nostalgia for Earth—where many of us, except shipped-in UD workers, have never been—it just looks tacky.

We dock at the arrival bay. The whole of Mining Compound 6 is dwarfed by the dome, lying, quite literally, entirely within its shadow. LMS's algorithm must be quite certain that they will find something worth digging up here to put up with that tension.

The transport cost is charged not to my private Universal Account, but Liberty Mining & Services. At the visitor centre, I'm greeted by a drone in its LMS-issued spacesuit uniform.

"No suit detected. Suit up, please." The drone's voice is metallic, breaking up slightly, even through my top-of-the-line comms. Must be using an older system that doesn't recognise my suit yet.

"This is a nude-suit," I say.

"You cannot be nude. You must wear a suit."

"I'm wearing one."

"Could you rephrase that?" asks the drone.

I sigh. "My suit's just a few millimetres thick. Like I'm wearing nothing at all."

"If I understand you right, you are saying that you are wearing nothing at all, and that you are nude. This is consistent with my assessment, which is why I require you to suit up."

"Check with Witsel. Override the requirement."

"In order to override the requirement, I require the 12-digit registration number for your suit."

I sigh again, this time at myself. I forgot to register the damn thing.

Many sighs and half an hour later, I arrive in the high-rise office where Witsel expects me, alongside a woman I don't know. Probably Human/Drone Resources based on how serious she looks. That is, until she sees me coming in, clad in a ridiculous faux-fur bath robe and connected oversized shades—the only registered replacement suit with good enough comms and display the drone could offer me—from the visitor centre's spa.

"What the Earth!"

"Your arrival bay drone gave me trouble over my suit. You've not got the new TesseRackT nude-suit in the database yet?"

"I thought we did." The woman frowns, then checks something in her in-eye display, the empty stare betraying her.

"We do have all TesseRackTs in the database. The drone's malfunctioning."

"Or it's picked up some rebellious behaviour somehow," says Witsel. "I tell you, look into that. The costs of all those retirements ..."

"Nonsense," says the woman. Good. I want to talk business. "I'm sending you the data on the drone that's giving us trouble. Lots of UniversalLang violations, but what took things over the edge was cryptic messages to another drone. Not only inter-drone, but possibly inter-zone ..."

"The Sinosphere?"

"Yes. But we're not sure about the contents. So, before you retire the drone, Jackson ..." The woman looks me right in the eye. "I hear you're good at investigating. Used to be in Free Corps Intelligence, even."

I nod.

"Just try and find out what you can before you retire the drone. About the messages. Whether we've been compromised. I'll give you access to its recharging station while the drone's at work."

"Just don't forget maintaining Turing-blindness," Witsel cuts in sharply. The woman looks daggers at him, sharper still.

"You'll be credited for your time." She sounds almost pleading. "I'll throw in something else. You can also retire that visitor centre drone that … embarrassed you like this. We'll pay standard rate for that retirement. I've just released the files to you."

That additional retirement does sweeten the deal, and I set off to do that first, and get my own suit back. In two minutes I'm a few floors further down, in a Human/Drone Resources office.

This is a standard retirement, so I can rush through most of the formalities. I skip the human-only questions. While LMS keeps stressing how important it is that the process be the same for drones and UD workers since the Human/Drone Acts, the only step that they mandate as imperative for both is the last question. In case the machines develop consciousness, I'm told. That's what Guelph's so afraid of. And what Witsel meant by Turing-blindness, I guess. Not heard that one before. Those nerds keep coming up with new words.

"So, your balance just now is 1,221 debits. We can release you from the drone-suit with that balance. Or you can sign up for scrapping, voiding your debit balance."

"Scrapping it is," says the drone. All drones do. No machine prefers the economically less profitable option. That's just how they're built. Honest in a way.

It's also the economically more profitable option for me. I get a bonus, so I quite like doing drone retirements. Discussing retirement options with human workers is boring, drawn out. They want actual counsel.

BACK IN MY NUDE-SUIT, downing my third can of coke, I catch myself whistling on the way to drone MCB-N2#42!x44's recharging station.

The door to the tiny room opens automatically. The drone works as a Drilling Location Negotiations Assistant. According to the information I've brought up in-eye, that job entails hammering out technical details of deals about drilling locations. Smart to give that job to drones. They won't want to know anything beyond the specific figures they work with, meaningless in isolation. And they tire less in trying to get the most out of negotiations with other corps or the Sinosphere.

What happened here then? Did this drone somehow become greedy? That would require consciousness. It's just not there. They don't need to make deals of their own 'cause they've got nothing of their own. The corps only keep track of their work credits to assess efficiency. Even so, some odd, unpredictable malfunction might result in such human-like behaviour. There must be some human data they learn from, otherwise they'd be caught in recursive loops. Which wouldn't bode well for negotiations—or any work really.

I plug one of my suit's adaptors into the backup memory connector in the bed-like recharging station. Whenever the drone is in the recharging station, a full record of its workday is uploaded to that backup memory, just in case of glitches or connection troubles with the online system. Also, this allows intrepid investigators such as me to check just one drone's data without access to the whole general system. Safer way to do things for the corps, and probably safer for me too.

This drone was flagged countless times for UniversalLang violations. *Ambiguous*, *Incorrect*, and *Synonymy* are the most frequent ones. The value of the relevant communications was debited to the drone's account. Could that have made a machine mad? That's paranoid. They're not conscious.

The drone's lifetime balance is 16,594 debits. Why did they keep it on for so long if it didn't score credits? A computing drone should do better than this. Guelph flashes into my mind. He's into ancient computing, ancient games. In those old useless games, the universal currency in future settings was usually credits. Nice prescience. If only those nerd losers had foreseen that in this golden future on the golden globe—golden sounds more promising than red-dust desert—they'd likely never see a single credit in their life, only debits. Computing drones are like red sand out here, as I keep telling Guelph. Real Mars men don't play games, they work hard, they hustle. I have to lean on him more. He needs focus in life.

I need to focus here too. My thoughts are all over the place. The coke is speeding up my neurons it seems like, but they lack direction. I open another can.

Let's see. It likely was the latest suspicious message that triggered all this. Who was it sent to? The Sinosphere, that woman said.

I bring up all the communications with the Sinosphere. The screen fills immediately, and keeps filling, the font scrolling in front of my eyes too fast to make out anything. Negotiating drones here must deal primarily with the Sinosphere.

I sort the communications according to number of violations, then filter so it just shows recent communications. This might be it:

The eagle will fly soon. You put it in the pen, I pluck it.
That works.

"That" is underlined in boldface. A comment bubble appears as I focus on the underlined word:

Antecedent unclear.

"Works" is underlined too. The comment there is *Synonymy.* Afterwards, every other word is underlined.

From my time in intelligence, I know that the UniversalLang translation and logging engine struggles with synonyms and unclear antecedents—the engine isn't aware of context. But this here reads like it's not even meant to be translated, logged, nor interpreted. It reads like code. But for what? Is this the revenge of the drones, or what? Are the drones becoming too human-like? I can't give LMS just such a vague notion based on vague inferences about vague nothings.

Damn, I have to piss like hell from all the soda. I shouldn't be doing those night jobs anymore. No, I should be doing them with Guelph. That's it! Teach him work ethic, make him spend less time with that fucked up old schooler scene. Two birds with one stone.

I make myself focus on the message again.

The eagle fz49ds ds893kmK

What? I shake my head, take another sip. Now it says:

The kD1m# fz49ds ds893kmK

The comment bubbles have disappeared too.

And why is there music playing? Softly, but it's getting louder. Unintrusive muzak, but it's getting more frantic.

Someone or something has fucked with my suit's programming. I better get out of it.

I don't hear the door slide open. I only sense something right behind me, something that the suit sensors haven't picked up. How can that be?

Then there's a short sharp prick in my back, not painful, just bothersome. Just like the fact that this suit is, for some reason, shutting down. I'm reduced to my normal senses. That can't be, shouldn't be. It means … nothing … then nothingness.

I WAKE UP RELIEVED. It's not that I've relieved myself while I was out—my bladder is still pushing, pressing against all of my insides. It's subconscious relief that my suit is functional again. Though I can't yet pinpoint why, things are different. I got a visor on this suit, for one thing.

What I see out of the visor is different too. I'm in … an office? It says "Office" on the wall. It isn't an office though. I'm sitting— you couldn't stand here, the ceiling's too low—on a chair in front of a wall. There's nothing on the wall but the sign saying "Office."

Something's ringing in my ear, a call. As I consider answering, the suit has answered the call for me.

The voice is agitated, high pitched. I don't understand a word of the language, but I can hear the speaker is annoyed with me. Then the translation engine makes the words appear in front of my eyes.

"Third time calling. Your drone-suit was offline, why?"

"Excuse me, who is this? You got this wrong. I'm a career counsellor, not—"

Immediately, my screen flashes.

Ambiguous. Unclear antecedent. Retirement counsellor is highlighted in red.

Incorrect! Use "drone."

Damn. It's a drone-suit. No, a simulation of one. Very funny. Disturbingly, my first thought is Guelph. Not him alone, but the old schoolers. This sounds like a stunt they'd pull. Put someone in a drone suit for a while, so they know what it's like to work like a machine. Or what it would be like for a machine if it had consciousness.

Violations: 150 debits.

Never mind that, I got to call Security. Luckily the suit's display isn't too different from my own.

"Security Department. MCB-S4#5aa6?2. How can I help you?"

"This prank's gone too far. They'll pay."

Violations flash up all over my field of vision. I don't care.

"Please rephrase."

"For fuck's sake. Get me Witsel. I'm a human."

Significant: Turing-blindness violation: You have broken the blind.

Please consult UniversalLang Manual for a refresher (NON-OPTIONAL).

REFRESHER:

This facility is completely Turing-blind. Human drones …

What? Human drones? The text continues to scroll past.

… must never break the blind when interacting with other drones nor staff, clients, or other contacts. No-one is permitted to know whether they deal with a machine or human drone.

Our clients like to feel well looked after, so would prefer a human contact; our competitors often feel they can cheat a human, but not a machine, in negotiations. And our management as well as all-human staff want to know they are not crediting a human when a machine would do, i.e. humans must be able to perform on the same level as the machine drones.

Relying solely on machine labour would result in a feedback loop; there must be human work involved as the basis for our machines to learn from. Those humans in turn must work with the same clarity and accuracy as machines.

Therefore, our policy is Turing-blindness. Human drones are required to conduct themselves in a manner indistinguishable from machines.

This also streamlines our business and language, including translation processes.

The fuck. The text continues rolling.

Ambiguities mean our TranslationEngine is at risk of choosing the wrong translation, resulting in losses; any potential such losses will, by way of precaution, be debited to the responsible drone's account. These are your credits/debits!

Unclear antecedents mean that context is required, and there often is no time for context; such potentially lost time will be debited to the responsible drone's account. Therefore …

Seriously? I can't read any more of this. I stand up before the text has finished scrolling. Damn, this suit is cumbersome and heavy.

I'm blinded by all the violations flashing brightly. Then they slowly fade into the background. Large letters appear on the screen.

EXCESSIVE VIOLATIONS. RETIREMENT IMPENDING.

The door won't budge as I hammer against it from the inside. Then it opens.

Someone's here.

"I'm your retirement counsellor." I know the voice. In the moment, before I can think, I'm proud of how Guelph's voice hardly shakes. It must be his first job alone. "Congratulations. We'll discuss a few questions."

"Guelph! It's me, dad! This is a prank gone wrong." A dark suspicion rises to the surface. What if he was, still is, behind the prank? In cahoots with the old schoolers? Do they know there are human drones here, too? He just stares at me as if I'd not said anything. Turns out I haven't. More large letters:

BREAKING THE BLIND IS NOW FORCIBLY DISABLED. IT IS IMPERATIVE NOT TO VIOLATE TURING-BLINDNESS WITH REGARDS TO EXTERNAL CONTRACTORS.

The suit muted the microphone. I scream, but no use. I flail my arms, but they do not move. The suit holds them in place. The visor must be opaque from the outside, as usually is the case with drones. Now that it's too late I realise why. The problem isn't that drones are becoming too human—it's that we've been making human drones, forcing them to become like machines. If Guelph thinks I was knowingly involved in this, then I deserve all this in his eyes. Fair enough.

Guelph isn't tripped up by any of the formalities. If that's a show for my benefit, he's doing very well. He skips the same questions I would. But not the last one. I told him how important that is to LMS.

"So, would you like to be released from the suit—with a balance of 16,594 debits—or a fresh start?"

My last chance, just in case it's all a misunderstanding.

"Please, Guelph! I never knew! God's honest truth!"

BREAKING THE BLIND IS FORCIBLY DISABLED. SPEECH SYNTHESISER ACTIVATED.

"Fresh start," a voice says, coming out of the suit, without me having any say in that. It sounds slightly broken, metallic.

This time, my son hears.

"That's alright, robot buddy, we'll download your software. Then you'll be scrapped." He chuckles. "My dad says all of you choose this."

The reluctant admiration in his voice makes me tear up. With the tears comes clarity: Guelph is innocent in all of this. He's a good boy—Witsel called him here on our business line. My imprisonment in this drone-suit might be some human drone's stab at liberty, a gambit to get me here, deactivate my suit, steal my nude-suit. Possibly with help from the Sino-sphere. Unlikely to succeed, but maybe it has. Or was it simply LMS wanting rid of me—did they think I'd learned something I wasn't supposed to?

Now I have.

Gregory Lawrence is an autistic translator and writer. Before he was confirmed as autistic, he was known only as proudly weird, and that sense of weirdness has also seeped into his writing. Apart from horror, speculative, and weird fiction, he is interested in heavy metal, linguistics, constructed languages, disability advocacy, and history. Originally from Germany, he now resides near Edinburgh, while his socials and words can be found here: linktr.ee/gregory.lawrence.

And I see you, unwonted sister of this era

by Stephanie Osuji

And I see you, unwonted sister of this era. How a woman can be what we call nectarine—a fruit from a period that has passed. All this time spent learning of history—his wars his politics his voice, the shape of his beard—What about her? What about the slight tangle in her valkyrie braids and the autumn brown of it, like a leaf passing onto the next season—this is what that leaf might've looked like if it hadn't died. Instead decided it could coexist with the cold, decided winter could pepper its blood with something like new life. What about the black of her eyelashes standing austere before the grey seashells that dot the Nordic blue of her eyes? What about what she wears—her clothes that flow like something that has flown or blown or known sometime before electric trains that coil around a house and snake through tunnels to take the half-metal bodies they carry to places unknown?

I would ask one day if I could just touch your skin, feel all of the human within. And you would only nod. But when I felt with my fingers the confession of the skin stretched tight at your cheekbones, she said, *Cold, smooth, blemishless, I do not crease, do not crack, do not cry*, she said, *Metal*. You, the beauty which hung before my eyes—these pupils piranhas baited by a worm writhing on the end of a rope. You are a machine like me. You told me women always were, even back then. I asked, *How much of you is metal?* You answered, *How much of me is woman?* I could see you were electric enough to coil around a house and snake through a tunnel to take a body that does not belong and make it into an epic an elegy a eulogy which seems to say I can see—the sad, the wonderful. I can see—the story of her.

When woman loves woman she tells her, the past the present the future are all happening at once. She tells her, it is much like those memories she still feels crawling carefully up the nape of her neck to insert fangs at the head. It is much like dreaming and dreaming and dreaming of the future until at last it has arrived and you can no longer spell out the time it took to get there—for your mind is already there. When woman loves woman she tells her, time takes its time cultivating mirages of difference and distance so that we can tally progress while we prettily sleep, sedentary.

Woman tells me: *You thought I was more woman than you.* Woman tells me: *We never escaped being machines.* Woman tells me her refusal to show the wires plugged into her head is her riot, her revolt. That her removal of the cyborg eye she attached when she was young, that is the flare she thrusts into the sky. That by the metal of her body made to look like skin she is Joan of Arc, leading her tangled valkyries to the Valhalla of the future they live within.

Stephanie Osuji is a student pursuing her B.S. in Kinesiology at Delaware State University. Her hometown is a small business area called Lanham, in a diverse district of Maryland. Growing up she was deeply invested in sports and general athleticism. She's a former collegiate athlete who has maintained an interest in training, reading, and writing. Her parents are immigrants from the Aboh Mbaise Community in Nigeria, Africa, making Stephanie a first generation African American.

The Wind Cries Electric

by Charles Chin

I found Sierra tinkering on the roof again, arms deep inside the airship tethered to the side of the building. The clouds gathered in the west, just cresting over the mountains behind the pillars of glass and iron buildings. Most of the populace would have hurried to their designated shelters by now, but not Sierra. I knew I'd find her up here, and I knew this would be the last chance I'd have to talk her out of it.

"Sia, we have to get to the shelter. The siren's been going for an hour."

She jabbed a metal probe into various slots, looking at the screen of her meter with a furrowed brow. "Yes, you need to get going. It's high time you left."

"This isn't funny, Sia. All the bulletins say this is the biggest storm in a generation, maybe since before the Split. We need to go now."

Sierra sighed and hung her head. "We've talked about this, Beth. I have to try. I can't lose someone else to another one of these storms." She turned and gently placed a hand on my cheek. The skin was rough, calloused from years of working on machinery, the creases perpetually stained with grease. But I didn't care. I grabbed at her hand, trying to pull the rest of her as well.

She smiled at me, a guilty smile, the one I'd see when she'd sneak an extra bite of my tart after dinner. She pulled me in for a kiss, one I realized too late was a goodbye. When she released, I stood dazed as she stepped backwards across the rooftop and onto the gangplank connecting the *Aurora* to the building. "See ya after this all blows over, B." With a two-finger salute, she pressed a button on her belt, and the walkway beneath her feet retracted. All I could do was watch as she closed the airship door and started the launch process.

"You damned fool." I didn't know if I was cursing her or myself. I never should have encouraged her work on the *Aurora*. It wasn't ready. We needed more time—for tests, certs, anything to make me okay with this reckless plan. But Sia wasn't someone who'd wait for perfection. I knew who she was when we met: a stubborn optimist. Someone whose mantra might as well have been "let's just see what happens."

As I watched the airship pull away from the building, I couldn't help but run through the blueprints in my head, my eyes scanning the lumbering machine. Sia would have checked all the levels before taking off—she was rash, not stupid—but that didn't stop my worrying. The great, rigid envelope of the airship reflected the evening sun like a silver mirror, the city skyline distorted on its surface as if on the back of a spoon. The shielded gondola hung underneath, a hulking mess of metal plates and chain-mail meshes. We probably should have put more care into the looks of the *Aurora*, but function always took priority over form.

The sirens halted momentarily, replaced by a robotic, authoritative voice. "ELECTRICAL STORM IMMINENT. PLEASE REPORT TO YOUR ASSIGNED SHELTERS NOW. ELECTRICAL STORM IMMINENT."

I glanced at the stairwell door behind me and looked back to the *Aurora*, already several stories up from where I stood. "Come back to me, Sia. Please." It was all I could muster before I dragged myself off the roof and down into the building.

Red lights flashed in sequence down the lonely shaft, stairs spiraling from landing to landing. Even in the confines of the stairwell, the distinct smell of ozone from the storm permeated the air. I should have been running down those stairs, but my legs were sluggish. There were a lot of floors to descend which made for plenty of time to think.

It wasn't that long ago when Sia dropped out of the sky in that pile of junk. I was refilling the hydroponic garden on our terrace when darkness suddenly engulfed me. Turning, I found an airship blotting out the sun like an eclipse, growing larger at alarming speed. I barely had a chance to step backwards before it came down hard, bouncing off the cobblestone before settling into place in the courtyard of our living complex.

It was in bad shape back then, rusted all over, parts obviously missing in what I hoped were non-essential areas. With a groan and a thud, the side hatch opened to reveal a well-smoked Sia, her smile beaming through the dusty haze.

"Well, what do ya think?" she asked, stepping towards me to give me a hug. "She's a beaut, right?"

I accepted her in my arms, but had trouble forming a coherent reaction with my eyes wide and my mouth agape. "The co-op is definitely not going to let you park that there."

Sia laughed. "Don't worry, already talked to the board. Took a few promises, rep markers, favours for a little handiwork here and there, but they'll let us keep it on the roof while we get her airworthy."

"We? Who's we?" I carefully approached the smoking airship, lightly tapping the hull with my toe. I watched in horror as the metal gave a little too easily. "Where did you even find this?"

"The reclamation yard down by the harbour. Just came in this morning! Had a buddy on the lookout for anything that'd fit the bill for our project, and what do ya know! Old reconnaissance airship, still working after all these years."

I chuckled. "You and I have very different definitions of 'working.'" As I looked over the heap of metal, I noticed a nameplate hidden among the rust, weathered from years of neglect. I brushed it gently with my hand, feeling the raised letters as they passed under my fingers. "*Aurora*."

A deep roll of thunder snapped me out of the past. I checked the number by the door I just passed. Eighth floor, still a long way down into the sublevels. The sirens outside wailed as the lights in the stairwell flashed, but my sense of urgency was gone. Knowing Sierra was out there in the storm sapped my will and made my knees turn to jelly. Why was she so stubborn? She gets something in her head and prods at it incessantly. But I suppose I wasn't blameless in this whole endeavour either. After all, I was the one who put the idea of fighting storms in her head.

How many years back I couldn't recall, but I remembered the yellows had just started sweeping down the forest leaves of the distant mountains. I brought Sierra a cup of tea and sat under the shade of one of the fig trees we'd trained to grow like umbrellas over the rooftop garden plots. Small purple fruits still dangled from its branches, ripening for one last harvest. Sierra had done her homework: the *Aurora* looked airworthier each passing day. With the rust buffed away and new panels in place, I started to see what she saw, the potential of it all.

"So, you fill the inside of the envelope with helium, right? That's what keeps it afloat?" I asked.

She took a sip of tea, admiring her work from the previous day. "Well, technically there are bags inside that hold the gas to make it easier to control. The envelope just helps give the whole thing a shape."

I puzzled over a thought, slowly uncovering an idea long dormant. "And you could make it out of anything, right? As long as it holds shape?"

"I suppose."

"So theoretically, if we sandwiched a thin-film dielectric between the metal plates of the envelope, the whole thing would basically be a giant capacitor, right?"

Sierra raised an eyebrow. "Theoretically, we can do a lot of things…"

"I'm just thinking, you wanted the *Aurora* to have a purpose. And the Council puts out a call every year for proposals around mitigating damage from the electrical. It's a long shot, but you think a capacitor the size of an airship could pull enough energy out of the air to collapse the storm?"

She set her cup down and stared at the airship, eyes twinkling, gears on her head already locked together and whirling.

"It's a nutty idea, Sia. Forget I mentioned it."

"No, no, B. Let's see where this goes…"

A bright flash lit the stairwell from the gap around the doors, followed quickly by another boom of thunder. The red lights cut out and left me in darkness. I didn't catch which floor I had made it to before everything went black, but after a few seconds emergency lights kicked on, the faint hue of LEDs through yellowed glass bathing everything in a soft glow. I found the nearest placard. Only on sixth? Had I really made so little progress? What would everyone think when they found my body up this far in the stairwell? They'd probably throw sad looks at each other and say things like *Bless her heart. I wonder why she didn't heed the warnings.*

Lightning flashed with regular frequency now, a timpani orchestra playing with increasing volume through the walls. The last electrical storm that rolled through the city blew out all the glass above three stories, took the grid down for months, and burned to ash any living thing unfortunate enough to be caught in the open. This one was supposed to be bigger yet, and of course, it's the one Sierra wanted to go against. She had that habit of going big, no way to steer her otherwise.

"I'm taking the *Aurora* up this season. She's ready." Sierra had spoken without looking up from the component under the magnifier, the rest of her desk strewn with design documents and schematics.

I had just walked into her study. "You can't be serious. She's nowhere near ready," I replied. She'd been at that desk for weeks, and I had come with a box of sweets in an attempt to drag her away. "Look, the equipment you ordered for the energy dissipation system just got here. All these boxes haven't even been touched, and you want to take that thing out into a storm?"

The soldering gun in her hand sizzled lightly as she set it down on a sponge. "She'll be ready." Sierra still didn't turn, her black curls concealing her face.

I set the sweets down on some papers. "Sia, Malcolm called me today. He said you haven't been showing up to the Institute. Your projects are missing deadlines. He's—we're both worried." Even though I couldn't see her face, I could feel the frustration winding up through her shoulders.

"Every season we delay is another season of casualties. I can't—" Sierra ate the last of her sentence and turned to me, her eyes a thin veneer between me and the simmering fury underneath.

I placed my hands on her shoulders. "You can't blame yourself for your brother. The *Aurora* was barely an idea back then. There's no way it would have changed anything."

"That's not the point, B!" she yelled as she stood, making her way towards the kitchen counter. "The point is, we have something that can save lives now. And if there's a chance that we keep even one person safe from the burning buildings, the uncontrollable current, the spontaneous—" Her train of thought ended suddenly when she slammed the cupboard door, the force shaking the mugs within. "I can't just sit back and hope for the best."

I walked around the counter and forced myself between her and the cabinets. "You can't take up responsibility for the City by throwing away the responsibility you already have to your job. To us. And I'm not going to sit here like some damsel while you go out there and get yourself killed."

She tried to avert her eyes, but I pulled her to me by the chin. "Sia. Do you hear me? Promise me you'll wait, please? Until we've had time to test everything. Can you promise me that much?"

Her face softened with a halfhearted smile. "Bethany Wong, always the voice of reason. Keep at it. One day I do believe you might just get through."

I pressed my forehead into hers. "That's a lie, and we both know it."

My foot missed a step, and I caught myself on the railing as the entire building shook. There was no lag between the lightning seeping through the cracks around every door and the thunder now, and barely a space between strikes. It sounded like a war zone, shells going off at every distance, rumbling vibrations bouncing through the metal handrail I struggled to keep hold of. I could feel the charge in the air pull at the hairs on my neck and on my arms, like the electricity was already coursing through me.

I dropped to my knees and wrapped my arm around the rail, trying to keep steady while covering my ears with my hands. The change in pressure weighed on my eardrums, as if the air itself meant to constrict me and press the breath from my lungs. I squeezed my eyes closed, but the strobe of constant lightning still seeped through my eyelids. My mouth opened to scream, but the storm drowned even the sound of my voice out.

I don't know how long I huddled there in a ball, waiting for the storm to take me. But the sound of thunder had unexpectedly softened, the light oddly steady. I stood, slowly, unsure of what this meant. Could it actually be the *Aurora*? Could it actually be Sierra up there, protecting me?

It was foolish, but I had to know. I needed to see that she was as capable as she thought she was. I climbed, one stair at a time, one landing to the next. My ears caught the faint sound of something new, something unexpected. It flowed like music, tones warbling up and down from above. I somehow moved faster going up than going down, each step hastening my pace until I was almost running.

I burst through the roof door to the sound of a harmonic tone, deep and electronic, filling the air. The wind swirled around me, and above, the sky opened as if I were standing in the eye of the storm. There in the center, I found the *Aurora*, still flying, a cacophony of light and sound that defied belief.

I stood stunned, taking in the strangely beautiful display. The airship glided like an iridescent jellyfish in a churning ocean. Long wires on rods splayed forth from the gondola like tentacles, swinging in the air as lightning passed in flashes from the surrounding clouds into them. The envelope was functioning as designed, pulsing white from the power held within. It was almost too bright to look at, a fallen star in a cage of electricity.

The tones emanated from the massive speakers installed on the *Aurora*. We needed to dump the excess energy somehow, and converting it into sound seemed one of the best ways to do it safely. The noise felt like singular and multiple notes at once, a harmony not exactly like music, but moving all the same. It rose and warbled, fell and held, the storm conducting a symphony for the entire city.

While I had known about the sound dissipation system, I didn't realize Sierra had also incorporated the extra systems

I thought abandoned. Massive sheets of bronze metal hung below the *Aurora* like kite tails, orange from the heat radiating off them. And in every direction, beams of light shot out, coalescent rods of green and blue and yellow laser energy.

It was sensory overload, a dance of lights and sounds that could be mistaken for the performance of an eccentric musician. But it was my Sierra, sapping the energy from the chaos of a raging storm and turning it into structured beams of light and harmonic music. I laughed, and screamed into the noise, a joyful shout of release. She had done it.

It felt as if the storm itself knew that defeat was imminent, and as the electric pop of lightning to metal slowed, the clouds faded into twilight. I could feel the static fall away from the back of my neck, the smell of ozone receding back to the wet aroma of the steel skyscrapers. The music waned like a bagpiper finishing their song, the laser show sputtered and grew dark, and the *Aurora* began a slow descent to my lonely perch above the city.

The gangplank extended onto the roof, and I ran towards Sierra as she emerged from the airship, steam rising from every surface. She removed the dark-lensed goggles she wore and smiled as I approached, the smug smile of victory. I didn't care. I flew into her, my head pressed into her chest, arms wrapped as tightly as I could muster. "You brilliant fool, Sia! I can't believe you did it. You beautiful, utter idiot!"

She paused before removing the earplugs from her head. "Sorry, B. I missed that. Did you say I was right about all things, now and forever?"

"I said you're an idiot!" I pressed a kiss into her face, unconcerned about whether I missed her lips. I looked into her eyes. They sparkled in the waning light. "Don't ever do anything like that again."

"Wouldn't dream of it! Now, I don't know about you, but I could use a drink and a snack. Is the pantry stocked?"

I grabbed her hand and led her off the walkway and back onto solid ground. "You know me, I always over prepare."

She placed a strong, reassuring arm over my shoulder, and we walked into the building together, under a clear sky.

Charles Chin was born in Oak Ridge, Tennessee. Raised by scientist parents to be a scientist himself, he needed a creative outlet to offset the rigid worldview of doctoral degrees and data science. He still writes about science, but on his own terms. Should you come across Charles in the wild, know that he prefers rum over whiskey.

Trifecta

by Adrienne Stevenson

I'm not sure what prompted me to put those goggles on. I really should have known better.

It was my first dig as team leader, and we had reached our target levels, below the blackened layer that marked the Great Change. I believe in the before-times they called this a landfill, but it was more a garbage mountain. The dig was part archaeological survey and part mining the past for useful materials—plastic, mainly. With every fossil fuel extraction site long defunct, this provided our only source of the raw material so useful in everyday life. So useful, and so profligately squandered by our ancestors.

It was my dig. With a touch of hubris, not to mention greed, I felt a proprietary interest in each unusual find. I let my assistants take care of the plastic and less common metal objects, to be washed and compressed into blocks for sale to artisans. I focused on items that might still function, or that could be auctioned to wealthy collectors. Even in these impoverished times we have a few. Most of their fortunes were made the same way I wanted to make mine—unearthing treasures of the past. Having already uncovered some ancient stone chess pieces, wrapped in opaque green plastic, I was eager for more. Each evening, after the team had departed, I stayed on-site, prospecting.

The strap appeared first. Faux leather—real would have rotted—in a rusty black colour, with detailed stitchery in a pattern of interlocking cogwheels. I scraped around it with my trowel, hoping to reveal a complete artefact. Gradually, more appeared, until it widened out and joined a more solid object. The usually compacted mass of garbage seemed looser here. I removed a little more debris, revealing a concentration of pale green plastic bags. Excited, I tugged gently on the strap. It wobbled. I pulled a little harder, and it gave. My balance lost, I fell back, and the dig face collapsed a little. I landed on something squishy that had also fallen, but that was common enough. I would look later to see what it was. Right then, the object in my hands seized my attention.

It was bulky, still shrouded in plastic. I gingerly peeled away a filthy layer, then another. It took me a while to understand what I held. The strap, joined to its partner by a brass buckle, led to an elaborately crafted pair of goggles. But these were no ordinary goggles. Not tinted against the burning sun, nor ground to correct vision. These were even more elaborate than the strap, and crusted with green-tinged metal devices, with hints of their original copper glinting through the oxidized layer. I noted several recessed levers, one that appeared to be a wind-up stem, and various buttons that I resisted pushing, for the moment.

The lens spaces were occupied by miniature optic devices about five centimetres in length. Were they varifocal? Magnifying? Distance viewing? Night vision? I suppose curiosity overcame me. It's as good an explanation as any. Even so, it was with some trepidation that I put them on.

At first, I saw nothing. Then, as if my wearing them had activated some mechanism, the lenses cleared, and I saw my surroundings just as I had before. Was this all there was? Warily, I felt along the right side of my head and pressed a catch that released the small handle, which I wound until tight. The goggles began to hum.

The sound made me shiver. What had I done?

Just as I went to remove them, the view before me shifted. I paused.

Flickering images appeared before me. A trick of the fading dusk? No, this must be a recording. Fascinated, I watched an indistinct figure appear on the viewer's horizon. This must be a telescopic function. As the person—a man, I thought—grew closer, approaching at a deliberate pace, the focal length of the goggles adjusted automatically. A mere few metres distant, he stopped abruptly. Had the wearer called to him? Without sound to match the pictures, I couldn't know for sure, but my apprehension grew with the length of his pause. So much so that every hair on my neck stood to attention.

Then he moved again, quickly this time. What did he hold?

The goggle-wearer stumbled backwards, throwing their hands up, obscuring my view of the man. Then there was nothing but sky. Grey, endless sky. So, the skies were occluded even before the Great Change. Now, it was commonplace, with rare thinning. Once, I even saw patches of blue.

I removed the goggles, and shook myself all over, like a dog trying to rid itself of water or fleas. Should I try another part of the mechanism? Perhaps not just now. Who knew what it might show? I was unnerved enough by what I had already seen. And then, I remembered my unpleasant landing.

Turning slowly, wary of what I might have sat on, I saw only another heap of greenish plastic, just like the material the goggles and chess pieces had been wrapped in. But the shape it covered was unmistakeable. A corpse.

But how could a corpse still be soft, after hundreds of years? And yet, our excavations had shown no signs of disturbance by a burial, so it could be no recent intrusion. Could these be the remains of an ancient murder, the one I believed I had seen? For I was in no doubt that the goggles had witnessed one.

The dusk had deepened enough for me to need my lantern. I hoped enough charge remained in the solar cell to enable me to complete the excavation. Cautiously, I peeled back the layers. A musty smell rose from the contents. What if there were still living creatures in there? I shuddered at the thought, but reproved myself for a hyperactive imagination. Even the cockroaches had abandoned this site.

I revealed a pale figure, naked, with clothing long rotted away. It lay on its stomach, back and buttocks waxy in the dim light. Adipocere. Corpse wax. Something I had read about, but never seen. Natural mummification.

I sat back on my heels, breathing heavily, but smiling broadly as I realized my good fortune. Even if there was nothing more to be learned from the goggles, this find was stupendous. But I was sure there was even more to come once I ran more tests on the marvellous goggles. My dig was fulfilling its promise.

Perhaps I should feel guilty about my delight. I knew I would be rich several times over, for I had unearthed a treasure trifecta: a rare artefact, a museum piece, and a story I could dine out on for years.

Adrienne Stevenson, a retired forensic toxicologist, lives in Ottawa, Canada. Her poetry and prose have appeared in over sixty print and online journals and anthologies worldwide. Adrienne is an avid gardener, voracious reader, amateur genealogist, and sometime folk musician. Her historical novel *Mirrors & Smoke* was published in 2023.

The Romantic Intrigue Beyond Worlds

by Mélodie Langevin

It was not the first time I'd landed on X34W-3. I had been to this planet before, witnessing its abominable events, but I had to return to preserve some more samples to present to the Mycelian Political Council and persuade them to intervene to help you stop hurting my beloved planet.

I am a Myceloid. My body is a complex structure of interconnected filaments, a kind of dark spaghetti portion floating in the air, surrounded by a veil of moisture. The physical form of my species is challenging to describe, and our definition of being relies more on the psychological aspect than the physical. We evolved to develop a collective intelligence, with each of my filaments acting as a processing unit that can communicate instantly with others.

During my previous visits to the planet X34W-3, I studied the fauna and wonders of life and fell in love with them.

I had the privilege of beholding the splendor of tropical forests, true jewels of natural balance. Within these lush ecosystems, I found the way each tree, each plant, finds its place in a biological choreography so impressive. It's wonderful to see how the different layers, from the canopy of the tall, majestic trees to the roots intertwined with mosses below, create a diversity of habitats that help regulate the climate and capture carbon. The symbiotic interactions between trees and mycorrhizal fungal cousins demonstrate an interconnection so enriching and essential to the health of the forest.

I also had the opportunity to explore grasslands and savannahs. I witnessed the dynamic interaction between herbivores and vegetation. Herds of wildebeests, gazelles, and other herbivores participate in essential ecological regulation. Their selective grazing influences the plant composition, promoting rich biodiversity and creating a balance between different species. There are also predators like lions who, despite their cruelty, play a crucial role in the food chain. I'd come to understand that this is commonplace on this planet, having observed the lives of many other creatures. Predators must kill if only to survive. This struck me as strange at first, given that on our planet, we live in peacefulness with other creatures and the concepts of hunting, predators, and prey don't exist. We live in harmony with the environment and practise advanced intelligent cultivation which is based on symbiosis with other forms of life. We have developed partnerships with plant and animal organisms on our planet, promoting mutual growth. For example, my filaments can contact the roots of plants, creating a biological connection that allows the exchange of nutrients, water, and information. I don't need to hunt to be fed. Even if the violence of the lions hunting disturbed me, I tried to remain objective and just observe the difference without judging.

Pollination, a phenomenon I closely observed too, reveals a fascinating intertwining between flowering plants and insects. I stood in front of a gigantic bed of flowers being visited by various species. Bees, butterflies, and other pollinators are messengers of plant reproduction. Their precise flight and interactions with flowers contribute to the preservation of the genetic diversity of plants. It is a natural ballet where every movement has a direct impact on the fertility and variety of terrestrial ecosystems.

As an explorer, I also ventured into much less hospitable lands, such as the icy expanses of the Arctic, where relentless cold reigns. My sensors capture the bite of frost, but strangely, I do not feel the associated suffering of this thermal extreme. Instead, I marvel at the austere beauty of this frozen landscape.

Glaciers extend over considerable distances. Their shades of blue and white result from compression and crystallization processes, creating a distinctive visual palette. Large fractures and crevasses, manifestations of past glacial and thermal stresses, pierce the ice. I observed polar bears and reindeer that have developed specific physiological features to withstand the cold. Icebergs with sculptural shapes resulting from glacier breakage float gently. Despite the climatic rigor, the Arctic exudes an undeniable majestic presence. I stood there as an impartial observer, noting the adaptation mechanisms and resilience of species facing the ruthless climate of this place.

My wanderings also led me to a radically different expanse, a beach where sand grains sparkled—they exhibited a characteristic light refraction under the weight of the sun. The heavy warmth of X34W-3's sun enveloped my filaments, creating a sensation both foreign and intriguing. The ocean stretched as far as the eye could see, a similar blue infinity captivating my ultra-perceptive gaze.

My filaments were stirred by the oceanic breath. I felt the breeze. Odor molecules from algae provided a novel sensory element to my perception. Contemplating the vast ocean, I felt the impulse of immersion into its depths, where the mysteries of the underwater world unfolded before me.

Marine fauna, with its remarkable variety, introduced me to a world where life persists despite the cold and high pressure of deep water. I visited the deepest point of the planet's oceans, more than 11,000 meters below the surface. In this dark, cold hole, strange creatures still find a way to survive. In the abyss, I saw bioluminescent organisms, translucent fish, and even giant amphipods. Closer to the surface, I discovered magnificent coral reefs. They reveal another facet of this ecological harmony. The corals, with their vibrant colors, seem to be the architects of marine ecosystems. In symbiosis with photosynthetic micro-organisms, corals harbor such exceptional biodiversity. Fish, crustaceans, and all other marine creatures coexist, each species contributing to the survival and flourishing of the entire reef.

What beauty! I was amazed until I discovered that all this sumptuousness was infected by a selfish mammal. Having further developed its cerebral apparatus, it began to build large things, and then it ran out of space.

According to the temporal calculation tool used by the parasitic mammals—as my species does not recognize the existence of time—I spent years observing the planet. At first, there were just a few of them, building little things to protect them from the elements, but they reproduced quickly. First a few hundred, then a few million, and now there are billions. I saw the destruction of my beloved nature by the parasitic mammal. Their growing brains enabled them to know and understand their planet, and so, with this knowledge, they believed they could control it, and became its masters, rather than live in harmony with it. Considering trees and animals as mere free products at their disposal, they destroyed without feeling even a little guilt for the life they were destroying.

On my first visits, I remember the planet being covered in greenery and natural spaces. Now, their gray buildings and roads cover almost everything, and there's very little territory left that they haven't conquered. And they've managed to shrink that territory. With their pollution, they've raised the water level, and many of the lands I'd previously visited are now submerged. They've even conquered the sea. I'd seen the appearance of an additional continent made up of their waste. Now there are three more such continents scattered across the oceans. They destroyed everything so quickly, in just a few hundred years.

It was too much—I couldn't let them do it. That is why I decided to compile a dossier to present everything to the Mycelian Political Council and see if an intergalactic mycelial intervention could be established to help the planet defend itself against the parasite.

Back on my planet, I relish being home again, but I have a mission to fulfill. I had to present the results of my research to my peers. The Myceloids, who maintain a life in perfect symbiosis with the organic environment, have founded cities whose structures emerge from the ground, forming a complex interconnected network. Each mycelium filament, acting as a biological conduit, carries bio-electrical signals allowing instantaneous communication.

The exploration of collective consciousness is a complex process. Gathered in specific sanctuaries, our filaments temporarily merge, forming a fleeting collective entity. This unique phenomenon offers us the opportunity to exchange and explore abstract concepts, and to deepen our understanding of the universe around us.

As a peaceful community, we adopt a conflict resolution approach based on collaboration. Disagreements are submitted to assemblies where ideas are debated, and solutions emerge collectively. The fabric of our society is interwoven with mutual respect, eliminating any notion of competition.

The "Guardians of the Roots" hold a prominent place in the Myco-council, embodying the living memory of our society.

Education is an uninterrupted process, with each individual encouraged to explore various fields of knowledge, contributing to collective intelligence.

Seeking to increase our knowledge, our arrival on the planet X34W-3 was the result of interstellar exploration led by 43B, a good friend of mine, aboard our organic spacecraft. These flying machines, born from a delicate symbiosis between biology and technology, allow us to traverse cosmic space and capture life signals emanating from different stars. The discovery of that planet, with its biodiversity and unique ecosystems, ignited a flame of curiosity in me, prompting me to undertake an in-depth study to understand the fascinating planet.

I shared my detailed observations on X34W-3's biodiversity, emphasizing the beauty and exceptional adaptability of the organisms that inhabit the planet before the Mycelian Political Council. I had to highlight the harmful consequences of the parasitic mammal, including deforestation, pollution, and loss of biodiversity. I argued in favour of a mycelial intervention to protect terrestrial nature against the destructive actions of 'the parasites.' Studying them, I learned their name, as they call themselves: humans.

Members of the Mycelian Political Council reacted with a range of opinions. Some were intrigued by the diversity of life on the humans' planet and recognized the value of its preservation. Convinced that Myceloids could bring beneficial support to the planet, they emphasized the importance of preserving biodiversity and protecting fragile ecosystems. Others raised concerns about meddling in the affairs of a foreign planet and the need to respect the free will of species. They expressed concerns about the implications of directly getting involved in human affairs.

In the days following my presentation to the Political Council, Mycelian society plunged into a period of intense debates and reflections. Ordinary Mycelian citizens, from all cities and generations, gathered to discuss these revelations. Spontaneous gatherings took place in dedicated spaces, where filaments mingled to share ideas and opinions.

I was the center of attention. Some saw me as a visionary, an ambassador of ecological peace, while others saw me as an intruder risking disruption to the natural order of things.

Facing this diversity of opinions and in respect of our traditions of collective decision-making, the Mycelian Political Council ultimately decided as a compromise to send a delegation of ambassadors to X34W-3. This delegation would be tasked with engaging in dialogue with human representatives, offering knowledge and technological support to encourage more sustainable practices while respecting the free will of the human species. I'm positive by nature, and despite the disgust I've felt at times observing humanity, I'm hopeful that you can manage on your own, without our help, and you still have the opportunity to change things. I'm writing this report on July 9, 2034, in your calendar. According to my calculations, you should receive this message ten years earlier.

Love can drive you mad, you know that. You can still live in communion with my beloved planet, just as any other mammal on it. You can also continue to destroy it, but … who knows what love will drive me to defend my beloved against your attacks now that I've seen the influence I can have on my people. We are normally peaceful, but we also know how to attack when necessary.

French-Canadian and a lover of languages and linguistics, **Mélodie Langevin** uses her mastery of words and languages to transport us into incredible fictional universes. After a career in administration, she quickly turned to writing and linguistics, unable to contain her explosive creativity. Passionate about philosophy, personal development, and protecting the environment, she includes these themes in her stories, making us think while entertaining us.

Universal Scale Factor

by Pauline Barmby

"**M**iss Johnson!" the professor prompted.

In the classroom's stifling warmth, Muriel had nearly dozed off to the sound of bees buzzing in the window frame.

"Miss Johnson!" he repeated. "What does the Robertson-Walker metric imply about the universal scale factor?"

Befuddled, Muriel made a helpless gesture. Her mumbled response was drowned out by her classmates' snickers.

The professor glared at her and raised his voice. "There are three possibilities for a universe obeying Einstein's general theory." He sketched a graph showing three curves, punctuating each in turn with a chalk stab that caused Muriel to flinch. "Eternal expansion at an ever-increasing rate. Expansion at a constant rate. Expansion that slows and reverses into collapse." Despite the heat, Muriel shivered as she imagined the future collapse of stars and nebulae imploding in a swirling maelstrom, or a cold, eternal universe drifting into the night.

"We will know the truth once the distances and Doppler velocities of the nebulae can be measured," the professor said. Muriel's shivers eased, chased by the warmth of a scientific idea. She could make those measurements. The future could be known.

THE ROAD SNAKED UP THROUGH the hills, more rutted and pockmarked with each turn. Muriel's joints ached from the jolts and her nervous stomach churned with the swaying motion. The motorcar rounded a switchback, labored up a steep hill, and lurched to a halt in front of a two-story stone building perched on a narrow ridge. The ticks of the cooling engine faded into an almost unearthly mountaintop silence. Muriel could hear her own blood rushing through her ears.

The driver shattered the stillness by clambering out to open the passenger door and breaking into a hacking cough. He recovered enough breath to announce, "Mount Carswell Observatory, Miss."

Muriel stepped out and exhaled in relief at being stationary. Above her, a dozen stone steps led to a massive wooden door, beside which a brass plaque proclaimed "Founded 1903." To judge by its gleam, the plaque must have seen daily polishing over the past two decades. The dark stone building, with its black-curtained windows, was a stark contrast. Just visible beyond a copse of dry pine trees were the gleaming white shapes of the telescope domes, rising above the trees and outlined against dark clouds that roiled with the threat of rain. Muriel's heart raced at the sight as she imagined herself using the historic Grand Refractor and the mighty 50-inch reflector to divine the fate of the universe.

Muriel's reverie was interrupted by the crash of her second trunk being deposited at her feet. "I'll be going now, Miss.

Enjoy your stay." The motorcar headed back down the mountain in a spray of gravel.

"Miss? Can I help you?" A sprightly white-haired and kind-faced man peered at her curiously. "I hadn't heard we were gettin' a new secretary." He doffed his cap and offered a hand. "Albert Morris, general handyman and all-purpose runabout, at your service. Welcome to Mount Carswell."

Muriel's back straightened with the familiar tension of having to explain herself. She shook Albert's hand. Her voice trembled a little, both timid and absurdly loud in the mountaintop silence. "Lovely to meet you, Mr. Morris. I'm Doctor Muriel Johnson, the new astronomer."

Albert's blue eyes widened. "A lady astronomer? You don't say! It's a pleasure to meet you, Doctor. I'll just go and collect the wheelbarrow to transport your luggage. But first I'll let the Director know you're here." Before Muriel could say anything more, Albert scurried up the stone staircase and disappeared through the wooden door. Her eager contemplation of the surroundings didn't last long before footsteps descended the staircase.

"Johnson?" a deep voice boomed. "This is … disappointing."

THE DIRECTOR'S DISAPPOINTMENT that Muriel was a woman, a fact she had carefully omitted in her application, was swiftly and volubly expressed. He objected to an unmarried woman residing in the dormitory and doubted Muriel's ability to endure long winter nights at the telescope. She tried to remind the Director about the hundreds of nights she had spent at the university's observatory, but he outshouted her timorous attempts to speak. The discussion was moved inside when the gray clouds opened up to deluge the mountaintop. The Director noted that the mountain road frequently washed out during rainstorms. Muriel would have to stay, at least for now.

Dinner took place in the office building's formal dining room, the table set with linen and china far beyond Muriel's

experience. Her discomfort was magnified by the gloom barely pierced by the dusty chandelier. At the table's far end, the
black curtains were drawn against the rain that battered the
lone window. Muriel was introduced to the observatory's professional staff. The secretary, Mrs. Green, clearly disapproved
of Muriel. The other astronomer, Dr. Sharma, seemed unsure
what to make of her.

Muriel was equally confounded by Dr. Sharma. She had
never met an 'Indian by way of Great Britain,' and she found
his accent difficult to decipher. Still, as they were both outsid-
ers, surely there was no harm in being polite. At first Muriel
responded in monosyllables to Dr. Sharma's interrogation of
her doctoral dissertation, gradually becoming more comfortable as she launched into a description of variable star light
curves. They soon discovered a mutual interest in variable-
aperture photometry. Out of the corner of her eye, Muriel
could see the Director observing their discussion with what
seemed to be incredulity that a woman and an Indian were
capable of such a technical conversation.

After dessert had been served and Mrs. Green had departed, the Director leaned back in his chair and fixed his gaze on
Muriel. "It appears, Miss Johnson, that you will be with us for
some time. While I believe your application to the staff of this
observatory was made under false pretenses, you do have the
qualifications to serve as a clerk. Until you can be transported
back to the city, you may earn your keep by cataloging our photographic plates."

Dr. Sharma had apparently made up his mind about Muriel's
qualifications. "Surely this is inappropriately menial work for a
scientist of Dr. Johnson's training," he objected.

Muriel agreed, but couldn't bring herself to cross the Director. "I don't mind," she murmured. Surely he'd let her stay once
he saw her skills.

"It is not a question of whether you mind," Dr. Sharma replied. "This observatory needs technicians, and as long as doctorate holders perform such work, the board will refuse to hire additional staff."

The Director stood, his face reddening. "Dr. Sharma. Let me remind you that I am the director of this observatory. You may have supporters on the board, but I make the decisions."

Dr. Sharma drew a breath and pushed his chair back. Muriel caught his eye and shook her head slightly. He took her hint and remained silent.

"I appreciate your finding something for me to do, Director," Muriel said. "Shall I report to your office in the morning, then?"

THE NIGHT FEATURED HOWLING WIND and pounding rain. Despite the supposed impropriety of an unmarried woman lodging in the same accommodations as men, Muriel felt secure in her cozy room, with its tiny windows and blackout curtains. She awoke wanting to know all about Mount Carswell, in the hopes that she might eventually belong here.

After climbing the creaking stairs to the second floor of the office building, Muriel found her way to the Director's well-appointed office. Sitting in the hard chair facing his imposing wooden desk, she maintained a neutral expression as the Director explained, "The photographic plate collection is in the basement. While the individual plates have labeled envelopes, the logbooks that record their contents were recently damaged and must be remade."

"All the logbooks? For the entire collection?" Muriel struggled to keep her voice from squeaking. The curiosity and confidence she had carried into the Director's office began to ebb away.

"Indeed," the Director boomed. "Plenty of work to do while you wait for the weather to improve. Mrs. Green?" he called. "Please show Miss Johnson to the plate stacks."

His failure to use her title had Muriel silently fuming. The secretary, equally silent, led Muriel down to the basement. Opening the thick wooden door at the base of the stairs, Mrs. Green gestured to one of three doors off the small square landing. "The plate stacks are through there," she said in an officious voice. "You'll find blank ledger books and pens in the desk. You're to work in that room only. Do not enter the other two rooms."

"Oh, are those photographic darkrooms, then?" Muriel asked.

"Not your business," the older woman said. She handed Muriel a key, turned, and marched back up the stairs. The door to the landing swung shut behind her.

The question of what observatory business could be so secret that it had to be behind locked doors promptly disappeared from Muriel's mind when she entered the plate stacks. It was impossible to resist pulling the plates from their envelopes, examining them on the light table, and marveling at their contents. Star clusters! Nebulae! Asterisms both familiar and novel! The heavens' beauty had first drawn her to astronomy, and she was soon lost to the world. When Dr. Sharma arrived to fetch her for lunch she leapt nearly a foot in the air at the sound of his knock.

As they climbed the stairs, Muriel asked him about his work. He described his spectroscopic measurements of nebular velocities in such technical detail that she had trouble following. Not wanting to admit her ignorance, she changed topics to enquire about the locked rooms. His response was polite but curt: "If you wish to stay here, do not ask again."

ON HER WAY INTO THE DINING ROOM, Muriel overheard the Director and Albert discussing a telescope maintenance issue. Her curiosity bloomed. Could she get her first glimpse of the beautiful machines? She'd come all this way to work at an observatory, not hide away in a basement. At the end of their nearly silent lunch, while the Director was deep in conversation with Mrs. Green, Muriel managed to catch Albert's eye. "Could I possibly come along?" she whispered.

"Certainly," Albert replied. "I could use an extra pair of hands."

With a quick glance at the Director, Muriel followed Albert out the door and down the stairs. On the half-mile walk to the domes, he pointed out everything from rocks on the side of the road to gashes in the trees made by careless drivers. "I've been here since the beginning," he said. "Even before the building sites were flat. Blasted them right into the mountain, we did. Ah, here we are. The Grand Refractor dome."

Albert let them through a small door into the building's lowest floor. Inside, thick silence and cool air swirled around Muriel. Dim red bulbs illuminated the narrow entryway. Albert proceeded to recount the history of the telescope, chattering as he led Muriel up two flights of clanking, openwork spiral staircase. He pushed open a solid door, gestured her inside, and turned on the lights as she gasped in awe.

The Grand Refractor was a beautiful, elegant construction, with a dazzling white tube perfectly balanced against the counterweight across its granite pier. Albert gave the tube a tiny flick, demonstrating the telescope's well-maintained bearings as it smoothly rotated into the air. "Would you like to see the focal plane?" he asked. Muriel climbed the rolling wooden staircase near the eyepiece and peered inside. The image seemed out of focus and she said as much.

"Aye, the Director said the alignment's off. That's what I need your hands and eyes for," Albert said. "It's a two-man, excuse me, a two-person job." He handed her a toolkit and climbed a ladder at the other end of the telescope tube. The hours Muriel had spent in her father's workshop and her experience with the university refractor allowed her to swiftly discern the problem. The process of aligning the lenses proceeded smoothly and Muriel felt the satisfying warmth of knowing that her technical skills were useful.

Courage bolstered, she ventured, "Albert, may I ask you something?"

"Of course, Doctor. Although it's clear there's little I can tell you about telescopes."

"Why did the Director tell me to stay away from the other rooms in the basement?"

Albert sucked air between his teeth. "That's … not something I can talk about. The Director's word is the last word here."

"What could possibly be so secret at an observatory?" Muriel wondered aloud.

"It's up to the Director, that's all I can say," Albert replied.

They finished their task and Muriel glanced at the dome clock. "Oh my goodness, I'd best get back to the plate collection!" She made her way outside, pleased to see that the rain had halted. Back in the main building, she descended toward the basement, passing Dr. Sharma. His only greeting was a muffled grunt.

Muriel unlocked the door to the plate collection room and began to copy dates, targets, and exposure times from plate jackets to the logbook. The methodical work left her mind free to wander, over Albert's reticence at the telescope, Dr. Sharma's chattiness followed by near silence, and the Director's insistence that she not enter the other basement rooms. The questions compounded in her mind until Muriel put her pen down and stood up. She'd been told 'no' so many times in her career and had only advanced by ignoring admonitions and following her curiosity. She had to know what was behind the locked doors.

The tiny landing was empty, the basement silent. Muriel tried her key on the middle door; sometimes the most obvious solution worked. Not this time. She collected a handful of tools from the plate collection room. After ten minutes' effort she had the feel of the lock's tumblers. Footsteps tapped at the top of the stairs, and she scurried back through the collection room door. The far door creaked open and slammed shut. Did she dare continue her attempts on the center door while someone might exit the other? Muriel attempted to return to her cataloging, thinking furiously.

After half an hour with no sound from the other rooms, she could no longer wait. She crept back out onto the landing and began to manipulate the center door's lock. Incoherent, angry voices sounded from the first floor—Dr. Sharma and the Director? Muriel scurried back to the plate collection.

The voices faded. Once more she stepped carefully to the center door and pried at its lock, stifling a victory cry when the mechanism clicked open. The door opened slowly. The room contained nothing obviously out of the ordinary: two wooden desks piled with papers and books, and a large chalkboard on the far wall. The meager light spilling into the room from the stairwell was inadequate to show any more details. Did she dare turn the light switch?

She did. Stepping further into the room, Muriel flicked the switch and examined the chalkboard. It contained a diagram plotting measurements of nebular distances against their Doppler velocities. She gasped. The diagram showed the unmistakable signature of a collapsing universe. The graph's slope implied a timescale not of aeons, but mere centuries. A universe headed for collapse in only a few human generations. *It couldn't be.*

Hinges squeaked behind Muriel as the door was flung open. A sickly-sweet smell filled her nose and she tumbled backward into darkness.

MURIEL WOKE WITH A START and banged the back of her head against a cold, hard surface. She was being held upright, wrists pulled away from her body. A lantern approached, lighting the gloom enough to show that she was in the Grand Refractor dome. The curved surface pressed into her back must be the cylindrical pier upon which the telescope rested.

"You wanted to see the telescopes," the Director said. "I imagine this is not the sort of intimate acquaintance you were expecting."

"What … ?" Muriel mumbled. She made fruitless attempts to yank her hands free. Despite the dome's chill, sweat began to trickle down her back.

"You were told not to enter that room," the Director barked. "Having seen the measurements, you cannot be trusted not to divulge them. An unconventional scientist like yourself would no doubt wish to let the world know of the universe's imminent and terrible fate."

"Why would you keep that a secret?" Muriel blurted.

The Director made a disdainful face. "The collapse is centuries away, and nothing can be done. Why let Mount Carswell take the blame for the news? Such publicity about the observatory would only open my directorship and past personnel departures to scrutiny, disrupting my thoroughly agreeable lifestyle. Better that some other observatory suffer that fate."

"What are you going to do?" Muriel cried.

"My dear Doctor Johnson. The arrangements for your unfortunate demise are nearly completed. A telescope accident. Crushed by an unsecured counterweight. Very sad." The Director's lantern flickered with his breath.

Muriel's fists clenched. She had not overcome so many obstacles only to die in satisfaction of this man's ego.

"I'm not the only unconventional scientist here. What about Dr. Sharma?"

"Ah, yes. Dr. Sharma's sponsor on the Board protected him for quite some time. However, Mr. Williams is recently deceased." The Director moved out of her line of sight. She heard a muffled thump and then a moan. The ropes around her wrists pulled taut.

From behind her came Dr. Sharma's voice, weak and hesitant. "Director? What is happening?"

The Director spat a flood of invective at Sharma. Muriel's face burned hot at the insults. She'd learned to shrug off unkind words directed at her, but to hear such abuse directed at another made her furious. Like her, Sharma had only wanted to pursue astronomy. Now he was unable to even get a word in edgewise as the Director detailed the plans for their deaths with something approaching glee.

The door opened and light spilled into the dome. Albert's voice echoed in the cavernous space. "Director? I have the dynamite you asked for."

"Thank you, Albert." The Director's footsteps crossed the room. "Let's just step outside for a moment." The heavy door slammed.

Muriel lowered her voice to a harsh whisper. "Dr. Sharma?"

A tug on her right wrist. "Dr. Johnson! I am so sorry you were caught up in this."

"Why didn't you warn me?"

"I did," he explained. "I hoped that you might be safe, if you did not recognize the discovery he was trying to hide."

"There's no safety here!"

"Neither is there any escape." Dr. Sharma's voice carried a tone of defeated exhaustion. "He has Albert, and Mrs. Green. We have no way to free ourselves."

Muriel's jaw tightened. Her head ached. "We have to!" she hissed. "We're the only ones who know the truth! The world must be warned!"

"What do you suggest?" His voice was weary.

"The tools I used to break the lock are in my skirt pocket. If you can reach it, we can cut through the rope."

A great deal of contorting followed. Muriel twisted her lower body toward Sharma until she thought her spine might snap.

The entire plan nearly derailed when Sharma proved reluctant to touch her. Muriel's frustration and terror overruled her manners.

"Don't be stupid!" she hissed. "We can be improper, or we can be dead."

He retrieved her small pocketknife and sawed through the rope just as the door opened. Albert shuffled through. Muriel circled toward where her other hand was still tied to Sharma's and pulled him toward the rope hanging from the lens-end of the telescope. Sharma grasped her intent, and together they hauled on the rope. The telescope arced gracefully. The counterweight swung in the opposite arc, catching Albert on the side of his skull. He slumped to the floor.

While Sharma freed their joined wrists, Muriel regarded the older man's prone form with some regret. "I'm sorry, Albert. You didn't deserve this."

"He was not innocent," Sharma said. "I realize now that your predecessor's 'accidental' hiking death was likely nothing of the sort. The Director could not have maintained the secret without Albert's willing assistance."

Muriel's heart pounded. It was difficult to know friend from foe, but she had no reason to doubt Dr. Sharma. It seemed their fates were entwined. They hurried down the dark staircase.

A flickering light illuminated the Director, ascending with a lantern in one hand and a pistol in the other. They met him on the landing between the first and second stories. "How … never mind, it's too late for you now."

Muriel released her fury at this man who had treated her and Dr. Sharma so poorly, who had perverted the very science she loved so much. Occupied in anticipation of his victory, the Director didn't notice Muriel's fist swinging toward his temple. When he saw her blow coming, he wavered between dropping the pistol or the lantern. Too late. Her blow connected and the Director dropped to the floor. Sharma used the rope still dangling from his own wrist to tie the Director's hands behind him.

Muriel scooped up the pistol. They descended the last set of stairs and crashed outside, panting.

Sharma led her toward a low outbuilding between the two domes. "With the car, we can outrun them." He seemed oddly hesitant.

"What are we waiting for, then?"

"I ... cannot drive," he admitted.

Muriel nearly laughed, he was so serious. "Is that all? I can. Let's go!"

The flight down the mountain tested Muriel's inexpert driving skills. Deep furrows trapped the car's wheels several times. Getting out to push, Dr. Sharma uttered some words in his native tongue that Muriel suspected were inappropriate for polite company.

At the base of the mountain, she stopped the car. Its engine hissed and ticked as she briefly rested her forehead on the wheel. She turned to face Dr. Sharma. His lips drew back in a small smile.

"We made it," she panted. An answering smile appeared on her own lips.

"Thanks to you."

"So what do we do now?"

His smile faded. "As you said, we must tell the world the grim news. It is only right that humanity knows of the fate awaiting our descendants."

"And makes the best possible use of the time remaining," she added.

"You are an optimist, Dr. Johnson."

"It's always been my only choice," Muriel said. She started the car.

Pauline Barmby (she/her) is an astrophysicist who reads, writes, runs, knits, and believes that you can't have too many favorite galaxies. Her fiction has appeared in *Nature: Futures, Utopia Science Fiction*, and *OnSpec,* and in multiple anthologies. She lives in London, Canada, and hopes to someday visit her namesake main belt asteroid, minor planet 281067. Find out more at her website, www.galacticwords.com.

A Side of Spinach

by Mahaila Smith

A small, silver-wrapped chocolate sat on Judy's desk. "Huh," she said to herself. She picked up the chocolate, unwrapped it, and put it on her tongue. It melted slowly. Caramel.

She tossed the wrapper into the dustbin. Straightened the files on her desk and put away her folder of copies. She picked up her bag and left, turning off the light. She locked her door and began walking down the passageway to the sleeping quarters.

Her room was in the second ring of sleeping quarters. Slim and short, it held just a coffin bed, a chamber pot, a wall-mounted radio, a small kitchen unit with a kettle, a cupboard of nutrient powders, and a food printer. She ducked into the space, climbed the short ladder, and stretched across the coffin, exhaling slowly. She thought about what to print tonight. She had some packets of dehydrated roast beef, peas, carrots, and mash. She pulled the cookbook from between her mattress and the wall and thumbed through the index, finding the page for roast beef dinner. She checked the proportions for each ingredient.

½ a packet of Roast Beef
1 packet of Carrots 'n' Peas
1 packet of Mash

She found the packets in her cupboard and added them to the printer. She added a tick to the army of black ticks in the margin of the recipe and put the book away. In less than a minute, the meal was cooked. The printer expelled it onto a pastel pink plastic plate with a matching knife and fork. The peas and carrots were neon bright and the top of the slice of roast beef was etched with deep, symmetrical grill lines.

She held the plate on her knees, feeling satisfied by the healthfulness of her meal. Some people would eat the addictive Meal-in-One bars whenever they were hungry. *Those people* had no idea how to enjoy proper food. She sawed at the stiff meat with her plastic fork and placed a piece on her tongue. Her room was silent.

THE NEXT DAY, SHE WOKE to the familiar shaking of the coffin. A man's cheerful voice said, "Good morning, Buttercup, time to get up!"

She sat up and slid out to the floor. She picked up her shower bag, her chamber pot, and closed the door behind her. It was a rule that all chamber pots were dropped off every morning for health monitoring. She stood in line behind the thrall of bleary-eyed passengers, each dropping off their plastic boxes at the clinic window. She was proud of how healthy-looking her waste was, clear proof of her superior dietary regimen.

"Thank you, Judy554," an automated voice said as she dropped hers off on the counter.

Then she walked to the bath. In the changing room she stripped off and hung her clothing on a section of the wall of hooks. She followed a crowd of women to the bathing room. They stood in the blank white sink as sprays of warm water, lotion, and floral scent were misted onto their bare skin. She stared at the bodies around her. Wide, thin, pink, and brown. The bath stopped and they stepped back to the changing rooms to get ready. Judy chose a standard issue sensible brown skirt and blazer from the rack of cleaned clothes. She pinned the dry, white rose her mother had given her before she left to its lapel. Then she walked to her office.

Judy was a typist. Every day she sat at a desk as her boss, Mr. Rudyard, dictated the messages that would be broadcast to extraterrestrials that evening. Sometimes she listened to the broadcasts, but usually she would be so bored from hearing them all day that she wouldn't bother. When she arrived, Mr. Rudyard was there, waiting for her.

"Good morning, Miss Moneypenny," he said.

"It's Judy, sir," she replied.

"Just a joke, dear, from back on Earth," Mr. Rudyard said, laughing to himself, "though I suppose that's a bit before your time."

"Oh. Of course, sir," she said, laughing uncomfortably.

"Shall we begin?" he asked.

Immediately, Mr. Rudyard began dictating from his spiral-bound notebook, and she typed the words on her portable red typewriter.

"We offer you food, hospitality, friendship, history, and culture," he read. "We are an advanced race of sentient life." Judy paused.

"Perhaps we should say 'species,' sir?"

"We are all members of the human race, Judy, I see no problem with the word."

"But the aliens…"

"Extraterrestrials."

"But the extraterrestrials may think we are … *prejudiced*. And if they think we are prejudiced against our own species, they may think we'll be prejudiced against them."

At that point, Jeremy had arrived with the morning snack of rice cakes and tea. "Hello." He nodded to them, placing the tray of snacks and the two green plastic mugs in front of them.

"Well, fine then." Mr. Rudyard sighed. "Change it to species." Judy beamed.

On her lunch break, she ate in the galley with other working women. She noticed, with contempt, that she was the only one who had chosen the side of spinach. She had become so quick at picking up the splashes of colour on each plate from a distance, identifying what food they denoted and storing that information for later. She felt like a camera, taking in all these women and their bad choices.

At the end of the day, Mr. Rudyard left early, leaving her to file the day's records. Jeremy came in.

"I thought that was really clever, what you said today, about prejudice."

"Really?" she asked, smiling at him.

"I did," he said, taking her hand and pressing something into it. She looked at it. It was another small, foil-wrapped chocolate.

"Oh Jeremy," she said. "It's you. You shouldn't have."

"I wanted to," he said. "You're not like the other girls. You're the only one who misses our home as much as I do." He lightly touched the rose on her lapel.

"Thank you," she said. "That's really sweet."

"Will you go out with me?" he asked.

"Oh … Jeremy," she stammered, "this is … surprising. I don't know what to say." He looked at her expectantly. "I'm sorry, it's just, well, we barely know each other. What if, instead, we spent more time together, first. We could have dinner, maybe?"

"Sure, that would be fine," Jeremy said.

"What about tonight?" Judy asked. "I was going to go to my room and listen to the broadcast."

"You could come over to mine. It's a bit cramped because I share the space with Eustace547, but I'm sure he would be fine with you coming."

"Great!" They walked together to Jeremy's room in the third ring.

Jeremy and Eustace's room was almost identical to Judy's, except there were coffins on either side of the kitchen unit.

"Hi, Eustace," she said brightly as they arrived. "I think we met at an introductory training course on Earth."

"Hi, Judy," Eustace said dejectedly from his coffin on the right side of the room.

"Don't mind him," Jeremy said. "He's just homesick." He turned to Eustace. "We're going to put on the radio, if that's okay?" he asked.

"Fine," Eustace replied.

There wasn't enough space for the two of them to stand, so Jeremy suggested she sit on his coffin while he printed their meals. "Did you eat already?" he asked his roommate.

"Not hungry," Eustace said, facing the wall.

She watched anxiously as he chose some packets out of the cupboard, turned on the printer, and fed them through. He brought her soap-pink salmon, electric green beans, and a glob of rice mush.

"Salmon! I haven't had salmon in months," Judy said. "You shouldn't have."

"It's no trouble," Jeremy said. "I still have lots." She wondered what he had been eating instead. He climbed up the ladder and sat beside her, flicking on the radio with his elbow.

"… clean teeth for clean smiles," the broadcast advertisement jingled, then the evening show began. "Ladies and gentlemen of the H.M.S.S. *Freya*, tonight we broadcast our message to the vast, open galaxy, in the hope of discovering other sentient life to advance the progress of mankind." Judy and Jeremy cheered along with the studio audience. "To all extraterrestrials…"

The address was fairly standard. When the announcer reached the section on the "human species" Judy gripped Jeremy's hand, and they smiled at each other. Jeremy turned off the radio when the program ended.

"Well, that was really lovely," Judy said. "Thank you."

"It was my pleasure," Jeremy said, stepping down the ladder, Judy following behind. He stepped out of the room, to let her leave, and began walking with her down the corridor. They paused at the pocket doors. "Is it alright if I kiss you?" Jeremy asked.

"Alright," Judy said. Jeremy leaned towards her and pressed his lips on hers. She hoped for tingles and butterflies, but instead, felt nothing. He stepped back and said goodnight. She turned and walked down the corridor.

She walked past the observation deck and stood for a moment, looking through the portholes at the eternal night. Earth was barely visible from here, just a bluish dot among the darkness. She stared and could hardly remember the feeling of grass or the smell of wet dirt.

Then a yellow ring with a blue centre filled the frame. It looked like the eye of a dead fish. The concave glass morphed its shape, and for a breath it looked almost human, until it dilated, iris contracting mechanically, like a camera lens. She jogged closer and pressed her hands on the wall surrounding the glass. In a blink, the shape was gone.

Mahaila Smith (any pronouns) is a young femme writer, living and working on the traditional territory of the Algonquin Anishinabeg in Ottawa, Ontario. They are one of the co-editors for *The Sprawl Mag*. They like learning theory and writing speculative poetry. Their debut chapbook, *Claw Machine*, was published by Anstruther Press in 2020. Their second chapbook, *Water-Kin*, was published by Metatron Press in 2024. Their novelette in verse, *Seed Beetle*, is forthcoming with Stelliform Press in spring 2025. You can find more of their work on their website: mahailasmith.ca.

SpaceKitty Adventures #42: Dogged Pursuit!

by Marc Fleury

*T*he story so far:

Our intrepid heroes, SpaceKitty and Ribbid, made a daring escape from the ancient catacombs of the Panthera system. After resuming their long journey to Ribbid's homeworld in the Swamp Nebula, they found themselves hounded by bot-controlled dogfighters at every turn. We now rejoin the adventure as SpaceKitty tries to outmaneuver her relentless pursuers…

SPACEKITTY YOINKED HARD left on the *Tenth Life*'s control yoke. Red laser bolts grazed its silvery hull. If the ship had whiskers, they would have been singed right off.

"Status report, Ribbid!" SpaceKitty yelled into the comm panel. "It's getting hairy up here!"

Ribbid's distorted voice croaked through the speakers. "The FRAP engine will be back online in an hour."

The Frenetic Random Activity Period engine was the only way to make the jump to hyperspace. But a busted anatidaen control valve meant they were sitting ducks. And that was just when the K-bot Retriever ship showed up.

Another round of laser bolts blasted at the *Tenth Life*. This time, SpaceKitty didn't react fast enough, and the ship quaked from the impact.

SpaceKitty pulled sharply on the yoke, but the ship listed to port, barely pitching at all. On the status display, the port-side quarter booster flashed red. SpaceKitty slammed her paw on the control override and transferred power to the remaining three boosters. She straightened out the ship and dragged the aft viewfeed onto the main display.

The K-bot ship fired again. Why were they still chasing? Sure, spacenip was illegal in this sector, but it wasn't worth killing over! Besides, SpaceKitty had dumped that spacenip at Ribbid's insistence. Well, most of it.

SpaceKitty ducked and weaved, and the *Tenth Life* moved with her like a second skin. But she wouldn't be able to keep this up much longer. The pursuing ship was a fully automated Retriever-class K-bot. It had no lifeforms aboard to slow down reaction time or limit acceleration. It was nothing but laser cannons and FRAP engines vacuum-welded to a hyper-quantum computer core. By comparison, SpaceKitty's ship was a toothless old stray with no claws.

An idea hit SpaceKitty like a rogue meteor. Of course—claws! It was so obvious.

"Buckle up, Ribbid! It's time for zoomies!"

"Zoomies?" Ribbid said through the comm panel. "What? Only the FRAP engine can safely harness the power of zoomie particles. It's offline!"

"I'm diverting the zoomies to the navigational boosters."

"You're *what?* Absolutely not, SpaceKitty! The ship will get torn apart faster than—"

"SpaceKitty out!" she said, flicking off the comm switch.

One paw on the yoke and one on the control override, SpakeKitty clawed in the commands for spaceturbo mode. The boosters shuddered from the overwhelming power of the zoomie particles. SpaceKitty struggled to maintain control of the *Tenth Life* as its speed doubled, then tripled. The image of the Retriever receded on the main display, but that wouldn't last. Within seconds, neon pulses flashed and flared from the pursuing ship's secondary drives. The K-bot Retriever began closing the distance.

"That's right, come and get me," SpaceKitty whispered, whiskers twitching.

On the main display, the image of the K-bot ship loomed menacingly as it bore down on the *Tenth Life*. SpaceKitty kept accelerating, pushing her engines to their absolute limit, then beyond. The bridge consoles vibrated violently as the ship strained against the solar wind. Even then, the K-bot Retriever gained on them.

"Closer … closer …"

SpaceKitty slowly moved her paw to the anchor controls.

"Almost there … Just a little more …"

The bridge hatch burst open. SpaceKitty let out a surprised, involuntary, "Mrowr?"

Ribbid stood in the open hatchway. Beads of sweat and swamp water glistened on his dark green skin, reflecting the insistent flashing lights from the proximity alert panel. "Space-Kitty, you're tearing the ship apart! Stop this right now!"

"That's exactly the plan, Ribbid! Strap in or you'll be nothing but frog guts on the solar windshield in about five seconds!"

Ribbid croaked in frustration and hopped into the copilot seat. "Doggit, SpaceKitty, how many times do I have to tell you? I'm an alien, not a frog!"

"Yeah, yeah, you toad me."

SpaceKitty jammed her paw into the space-anchor control module.

Ribbid tightened his seat harness. "I strongly advise that you reconsid—"

SpaceKitty extended the Claws.

The anchor points of the ship's Claws ripped into the luminifeline aether like an ambush of tigers pouncing on a cardboard box. The fabric of spacetime itself shredded into nothingness as the *Tenth Life* spun out crazily, ripping reality, reducing all nearby matter into its component furmions.

Unable to change course in time, the K-bot Retriever barrelled into the disintegrating aether. The ship split into ten thousand silicon shards, and each fragment imploded and winked out of existence.

SpaceKitty pumped her paw in the air. "Yeah! Took 'em to the Vet!"

Ribbid was too busy checking system status reports to celebrate. "Doggit, SpaceKitty, you could have destroyed the whole ship with that maneuver."

"Well, it is *my* ship."

"But I'm on it!" Ribbid protested. He sighed at the damage reports. "This is going to take even longer to repair than the FRAP engine."

"Oh, quit your chirping, Ribbid. I had to do *something*. We were about to be blasted into spacedust."

"I just can't figure out how they found me."

SpaceKitty frowned. "What do you mean 'found you?' I thought you said they detected remnants of the spacenip we had to dump."

"Ah … right. Yeah. It was … the, uh … the spacenip."

Not for the first time, SpaceKitty wondered if Ribbid was being completely honest with her. She never did find out the meaning of that coded message he received from the mysterious "Thad Pohl," but now wasn't the time to get into that.

Ribbid snapped his tongue at the status display. "The exhaust ports are covered in toxic plasma. We need to get planetside for repairs."

"I'm detecting an inhabited world in the system," SpaceKitty said. "Advanced species, felinoid. We should be able to get what we need there."

"In this system? That can't be right. The Spaceopedia shows no record of fur-bearing lifeforms here."

SpaceKitty shrugged. "Ship's scentsors say otherwise. I'm taking us in."

Ribbid unfastened his harness. "I need to remoisten in my liquipad. Please be careful, SpaceKitty. There's something strange going on—that planet shouldn't even exist."

"I'm sure it will be fine, Ribbid. Stop being such a worrywart."

As the *Tenth Life* approached the uncharted world, SpaceKitty felt confident that nothing strange or exciting would happen on this planet. It would all be fine. Just fine…

What untold dangers lurk on this mysterious planet? Will our heroes survive their treacherous trek through dog-controlled space? And will SpaceKitty ever find out who put that cucumber in her spacefridge?

Find out next week, in another thrilling episode.

SpaceKitty Adventures #43: Planet of the Hominoidea!

Marc Fleury is a writer living near Kingston, Ontario. In a previous century, he wrote comic books. More recently, his short stories have appeared in *ZNB Presents* and *Seize the Press.* Marc can sometimes be found sitting on a park bench staring into the middle distance. He doesn't play hockey.

About the Editor

Libby Graham (she/her) is a UFO enthusiast and co-editor of *The Sprawl Mag*, a (cyber-)feminist, anti-colonial magazine focused on publishing diverse voices in sci-fi and fantasy. She lives with her girlfriend in friendly Manitoba, on Treaty One territory. Her work has appeared in *Radon Journal, Star*Line*, and other venues.